CANTINA SHOOT-OUT!

"Give me a shot of tequila," Slocum ordered in English.

The bartender reached for a bottle and a glass, then poured the drink. He slid the glass across the bar to Slocum.

Slocum started to reach for his money. Then, out of the corner of his eye, he saw that the border jumper at the table was standing up with his pistol in his hand. Slocum slipped his own pistol out quick as a snake, and he and the other American stood facing each other, pistols drawn.

"You can talk or you can die," Slocum said quietly. He didn't have to speak loud, because every voice in the cantina fell silent when the men faced each other over drawn guns.

The quiet room was shattered with the roar of two pistols exploding. The Mexicans yelled and dived, scrambling for cover. White gunsmoke billowed out in a cloud that filled the center of the room, momentarily obscuring everything...

OTHER BOOKS BY JAKE LOGAN

JAKE LOGAN

SEVEN GRAVES
TO LAREDO

BERKLEY BOOKS, NEW YORK

SEVEN GRAVES TO LAREDO

A Berkley Book/published by arrangement with
the author

PRINTING HISTORY
Berkley edition/January 1987

ISBN: 0-425-09479-0

A BERKLEY BOOK ® TM 757,375
Berkley Books are published by The Berkley Publishing Group,
200 Madison Avenue, New York, NY 10016.
The name "BERKLEY" and the stylized "B" with design are
trademarks belonging to Berkley Publishing Corporation.

PRINTED IN THE UNITED STATES OF AMERICA

1

The tall man sat in his saddle on the south side of the Salado and watched as Pedro Gallinas drove the eight purebred horses across the river. They were magnificent animals with coats so lustrous black that the light that played off them danced with blue highlights. The horses crossed the water with tails and manes flying, heads held high, nostrils flaring, and slender but powerful legs kicking up sheets of silver spray.

John Slocum took a long pull from his canteen, corked it, and hooked it back on the pommel of his saddle. He looked at the horses, their coats shining with spray, gleaming in the sun. If there was anything more beautiful in nature than healthy, purebred horses cavorting in a fast-running stream, he didn't know what it was. How could anyone be exposed to these magnificent creatures and not be stirred by them? And yet Pedro gave no

1

indication that the animals were anything more than objects to be moved.

Pedro glanced over in Slocum's direction, but said nothing.

That was typical. They had been on the trail together for four days now, and the short, swarthy Mexican wrangler had spoken only when it was necessary. At night, Pedro sat quietly, cleaning the brace of converted Colt .45s which he wore high on his gunbelt. By day, the Mexican rode in silence, save for an occasional whistle or clucking sound directed toward the horses they were driving.

That was all right by John Slocum. He was pretty much of a loner anyway, and he could spend his time as quietly as any man. Anyway, this wasn't a vacation. Pedro had contracted for the horses from Slocum, acting as an agent for Don Eduardo Honorio Velazquez y Soltano, a very wealthy and influential landowner in northern Mexico. Slocum looked around all over west Texas until he found just what Soltano wanted. The horses were quality mounts and the price was dear but Slocum paid hard cash for them. The purchase of the horses and what it cost to outfit himself for the trail down to the Soltano Rancho caused Slocum to spend a great deal of money. He wasn't concerned about it, though. He stood to make a handsome profit once the mounts were delivered and Soltano repaid his expenses plus the large fee promised him.

Slocum slapped his legs against the side of his paint and moved up alongside the string of mounts they were driving. The horses would be in Soltano's hands before nightfall this day, and Slocum, his pockets heavy with cash for a change, would be on his way back to Texas.

That is, if nothing went wrong. John Slocum had been

around long enough to know that plans seldom went without a hitch. For some time now, he had been aware that two men were dogging them, riding parallel with them and, for the most part, staying out of sight. They were good, but Slocum was better. He was on to them as soon as they started shadowing the trail.

Slocum let it go for a period of time while he kept an eye on them. Finally he decided it was time to do something about it.

"Pedro," Slocum said. He moved up beside the Mexican.

Pedro glanced at him, but said nothing.

"There are two men riding alongside us."

Pedro looked around, then shrugged.

"I see nothing, *señor*," he said.

"Look at the notch in the hill off to our left. In just a moment they'll go through there."

Pedro looked in the direction indicated by Slocum, and, as John had said, the two riders moved quickly through the notch, slipping by so quietly and expertly that only someone who was specifically looking for them would have noticed.

"Did you see them?" Slocum asked.

"*Sí,*" Pedro said.

"Who are they?"

"I do not know, *señor*," Pedro said. After a moment, he added, "Perhaps they are Delgado's men."

"Delgado?" Slocum's green eyes narrowed.

"Emiliano Delgado," Pedro said.

"I've heard of him," Slocum said. "He's a guerrilla, isn't he?"

"No more," Pedro said. "Once, he was a guerrilla. Now he is a bandit. He is an enemy of Don Soltano. I think he will want Don Soltano's horses."

"Yeah?" Slocum said. A slow, ironic grin spread across his face. "Well, I got news for both Delgado and Soltano. Until I'm paid, these are my horses ... and no one is going to get them."

"They are very determined men, *señor*."

"So am I. Keep the horses moving," Slocum said. "I'll be back."

Slocum left the trail and, using a ridgeline for concealment, rode ahead about a thousand yards. He cut over to the gully the two men were following, then dismounted, pulled his Winchester .44-40 from its saddle boot, and climbed onto a rocky ledge to wait for them. He jacked a round into the chamber.

The place reminded him of Devil's Den, the rock-strewn gully at Gettysburg where, as a sharpshooter, he had picked off nearly an entire company of Yankee soldiers from four hundred yards away. This would be an easier shot, if he wanted to take it.

He didn't want to kill them, though. He knew there were times when one had to kill and when those times came, there was no place for hesitancy. He had killed many times since the War, and he knew he would kill many times again. But, as much as he could, he had made a compromise with grim reality. He killed only when he had no other choice. These two riders had not yet put him in such a position.

They really were quite good, he thought to himself. They approached so skillfully he could barely hear them. Not one word was being spoken, and the rocks which were being disturbed by the horses' hooves were moving as lightly as if they were being dislodged by some mountain creature. Slocum watched, then saw them come into view from around the bend. He stood up suddenly.

"*Carajo!*" one of the riders exclaimed in a startled

shout. His horse reared, and his hand started toward his pistol.

"Don't do it, *hombre!*" Slocum warned, raising his rifle to his shoulder.

"I would listen to the *gringo,*" the other man said. Both men were wearing large *sombreros,* colorful *serapes,* and crossed bandoliers bristling with shells.

"Your friend is making sense," Slocum said.

The one who had started toward his pistol stopped his hand, then got his horse under control.

"I don't know what you gents are after," Slocum said. "But I don't aim to take any chances. I got too much money tied up in those animals to let a couple of bandits take them from me."

"We are not bandits, *señor,*" one of the men said.

"Yeah, well, you're not buyers either, so I don't really give a damn who or what you are. I'm not taking any chances. I want you both to drop your guns and belts, then turn around and ride out of here."

"*Señor,* there are bandits in this country. It is not safe to be without guns," one of the riders argued.

"You don't say," Slocum replied. He made an impatient motion with the barrel of his rifle. "Shuck 'em," he said.

Grumbling, and protesting their innocence, the two men got rid of their weapons, dropping them onto the rocks with a clatter.

"You know where Santa Luz is?" Slocum asked.

"*Sí,*" one of the men said. They were both glaring at Slocum with open hatred. "We know the village."

"Why do you ask, *señor*? Are you lost?" the other asked. "I will be glad to show you the way."

"Never mind that. That's where I'm takin' your hardware."

"Que dices?"

"Your guns . . . *pistolas,*" Slocum said. "You can pick them up in Santa Luz. Now, get."

The two Mexicans turned and started back up the gully. Slocum fired at a rock very near them and the whining echo of the bullet frightened the horses, or the men, or both, and set them off at a gallop. He waited until they were some distance away, then picked up their gunbelts and draped them across the saddle in front of him.

When he returned to Pedro and the herd a few moments later, Pedro looked around at him.

"I heard only one shot. Did you kill them?" Pedro asked.

"No."

"I think maybe you made a mistake," Pedro said. "You should have killed them."

"I don't kill unless I have to," Slocum replied.

"But you are a gunman, *señor.* I have heard you are very fast."

"I don't have to kill everyone who braces me, just because I'm fast."

"You are too soft, *señor.* One day it may get you in trouble," Pedro suggested. "I would have killed them. They are Delgado's men. Delgado is our enemy."

"Uh-uh," Slocum muttered. "Delgado might be your enemy, but he isn't mine."

"I think now he is your enemy too. He knows you are working for Don Soltano."

"I'm selling some horses to Soltano, I'm not working for him. I'm not a part of this war."

"Delgado does not know this. You had better be on your guard."

"I intend to be. All I want is to get my money and get out of here. How much longer till we get to Soltano's place?" Slocum asked. He took the makings for a smoke from his pocket.

"We are nearly there, *señor*," Pedro said.

"Good," Slocum answered. He put the cigarette in his mouth, lit it, then let out a long stream of blue smoke. Pedro moved back over to the other side of the string of horses. This was the most Pedro had spoken in the whole time Slocum had known him.

Slocum decided he liked Pedro better when he was quiet.

2

The sun was high and hot. A young woman stood in the shade of a palo verde tree atop Sombras Peak, while behind her a palomino pony waited patiently. The woman was looking out across more than thirty-five thousand acres of the finest rangeland in the Mexican state of Coahuilla. Though most of the grass was browned by the sun, a long verdant ribbon, greened by the water of Soltano Creek, snaked across the valley floor.

On such a day as this, animals and people searched out cool areas for protection against the sun. Hundreds of little islands of cattle had scattered across the range to stand or lie in clusters around the trees and rocks which would offer them shade.

Before leaving the house Linda had filled the canteen with cool tea. Now she took a swallow as she stood here looking down on the ranch. How beautiful it looked. How peaceful.

But she knew it was all a lie. That such a pastoral scene would soon be shattered by range war seemed an insult to the senses, and yet her father was determined to bring that about.

She had hoped, prayed, that the differences could be settled without bloodshed, but it was a false hope. She and her brother had discussed their father and his violent ways, and they knew it would all come to this. And now, after what she had learned this morning, it was about to begin.

She sighed, hooked her canteen back on the pommel of her saddle, then remounted. She would miss this place. Ever since she was a little girl, when she had something on her mind or was troubled, she had ridden the trail up to Sombras Peak. Here, in the vastness of the land before her, whatever was troubling her would seem small.

This time it didn't work. For the first time in her life the problem she contemplated seemed bigger than the land. As she rode back down toward the house, her mind was made up. It wasn't a pleasant decision, but it was the only one she could make.

Chickens squawked and scurried to get out of the way as Slocum and Pedro herded the horses across the wide plaza of the Soltano Rancho and into the corral. A couple of men who had been lazing in the shade got up and walked over to the fence to look at the animals and they passed a few remarks between them, impressed by the quality of the horses. An old woman was drawing water at the well, and Slocum rode over to the well, then dismounted. Without his having to ask for it, she offered him some water.

"*Gracias,*" he said, taking the dipper. The woman nodded. As he drank deeply, he looked at her. At first he had thought the woman was a servant, an old peasant woman who worked on the place. But there was a quiet dignity about her that spoke more eloquently than words and which told him she was a lady of noble birth. It was, however, a dignity that had been sorely strained by time and events, and her liquid brown eyes appeared to harbor some secret trial. She seemed to realize that he was studying her and seeing much more deeply into her soul than she cared to show. She took the dipper when he was finished, then nodded at him and carried the bucket toward the rear of the large, colonnaded house which dominated the grounds. Slocum watched her walk away, and wondered what had so dominated her spirit.

From the front of the house a tall, dark man started toward the well. He was wearing a black hat and was dressed in black trousers and a black waistcoat. Silver conchos around his hatband and a red cummerbund relieved the somber color. The man smiled, showing even, white teeth against a tanned face. He stuck out his hand.

"Welcome, welcome," he enthused. "Welcome to the Hacienda del Soltano, *Señor* Slocum. I am Don Eduardo Honorio Velazquez y Soltano."

Slocum shook the don's hand, then nodded toward the corral where the horses, as if aware that their journey had ended, trotted around the paddock exploring their new home.

"I've got your horses," he said.

"Yes, and what magnificent creatures they are," Don Soltano said. "I watched from my window as they were put in the corral. You have done well. The six Americans I have sent for to ride with me will appreciate having such fine animals. As, of course, will I."

"That leaves one extra," Slocum observed. "A spare for you, Don Soltano?"

"No, *Señor*, that is your horse. I wish you to stay, ride at my side when we go after Delgado."

"No, that's Mexican business," Slocum said. "Just pay me what you owe for the horses and I'll be heading back over the border."

"Yes, yes, of course," Soltano answered. "But first, please, come into the hacienda with me," he insisted.

Slocum followed Soltano across the flagstone patio, under the adobe arches, then down a long, shaded walkway flanked by hanging pots of bright red geraniums. Inside the house the living room was cool and dark. A crucifix hung on one wall. On another wall, suspended by wires, hung a large painting of a Spanish nobleman astride a beautiful horse. Soltano went over to a highly polished table and opened a silver case, then offered Slocum a long, thin cheroot. He took one himself, held a match to Slocum's smoke, then his own, and let out a billowing cloud of smoke before he spoke again.

"Are you sure you don't wish to ride with me?"

"I'm sure. In fact, I'd like my money right away," Slocum said. "I want to get started back today."

"Must you be in such a hurry?" Soltano asked. "Can't you enjoy my hospitality? Something cool to drink, perhaps?" Soltano waved his arm around the spacious, well-appointed room. "As you can see, I have all it takes to make a man comfortable. I can offer you a most pleasant stay."

Slocum knew about Soltano, had heard about him before he took the job. Soltano was wealthy because he was the biggest thief in Mexico; a cruel landowner whose stature was gained solely by standing atop his peasant workers' shoulders in his polished black boots. Slocum had heard that Soltano was engaged in a bitter struggle with a smaller landowner who happened to control the water to a large portion of Don Soltano's land. When he first heard the story, he didn't know who the other land-owner was. He knew now that it was Emiliano Delgado, the tough Mexican-Yaqui, former guerrilla whose men had shadowed him on the trail. But that was all Mexican politics, and Slocum figured it was none of his business.

"No, thank you," Slocum said. "Just give me my money and I'll be on my way."

"Ah, that is not so easy. I have sent for the money, but it is slow to arrive. There are the bandits and the surly peons between here and Mexico City. One must be patient. But, if you want to ride with me, in a few days I will double your money."

Slocum bit down on his cigar and squinted through the smoke at Soltano. He was broke now, as a result of taking Soltano's word that he would be paid as soon as he arrived. He drew a breath to protest, but Soltano interrupted him as two women entered the room.

"But, *espera usted un momento,*" Soltano said. "I would like you to meet my family. First my wife, Esperanza."

Esperanza was light-skinned, with blue Castilian eyes. She was a small, birdlike woman, who moved with a stoop-shouldered walk. She glanced up briefly, then looked down again, as if unsure that she had the right to intrude, and she spoke softly.

"And my daughter, Linda."

Soltano's daughter glided across the room. Involuntarily, Slocum caught his breath. She was incredibly beautiful. She had the light olive skin of her Castilian forebears, the soft fiery eyes of a *Sevillana,* and the raven-black hair of Morrish ancestors. When she looked at Slocum, he could feel his blood beginning to boil, and she smiled, as if she knew every thought he was having.

"I am pleased to meet you, Mr. Slocum," she said. Her English was flawless, but her words were kissed lightly by her accent.

"*Señorita,*" Slocum said, nodding at her.

"Will you be our house guest?" Linda asked.

"Uh . . . no," Slocum said. He coughed. "I wouldn't want to intrude."

"Oh, I assure you, Mr. Slocum, it wouldn't be an intrusion," the don said. "There is plenty of room here for you, and Linda will make your stay comfortable while we wait for the money and the six *Americanos* from Laredo."

Slocum had no choice. If he wanted his money, he would have to stay and wait for it. But he didn't want to put himself in debt to Soltano. Though he didn't admit it, not even to himself, he also didn't want to put himself under the influence of a woman as beautiful as Soltano's daughter.

"I'll wait for the money, Don Soltano," he said. "I don't have any other choice. But I won't wait here."

Soltano sputtered in surprise. "But where will you wait?"

"There must be a hotel in Santa Luz."

"Yes, of course. Though it can hardly compare with what I have to offer you here."

"Don Soltano, I told you, the only thing you have to offer me is my money," Slocum said. He touched the brim of his hat. "*Señora, señorita,*" he said to the two ladies present, then added to Soltano, "I'll be in town."

Linda watched the interplay between her father and Slocum, and she found herself strongly attracted to the American. She was fascinated by his height, his green eyes, his muscular arms and wide shoulders. But there was much more than his physical attraction which drew her to him. Slocum was very much his own man, a man who refused to be manipulated by her father, despite her father's wealth and power. She knew that Slocum had irritated her father, not only by refusing to stay at the hacienda, but also for turning down his job offer.

Ironically, she had overheard her father talking just the day before. He said then that a gringo named John Slocum, a gunfighter, was bringing horses down to him and would join his band. When the person her father was talking to suggested that Slocum might refuse, her father had laughed and said that every man has his price.

That might be true, Linda thought, smiling. But whatever Mr. Slocum's price was, her father couldn't afford it. She liked that. She liked that very much.

Linda walked back to the kitchen and looked through the window as Slocum walked out to his horse. Esperanza came into the kitchen to stand behind her daughter.

"He is much man, isn't he?" Linda said to her mother.

"I fear if he is not careful he will make an enemy of your father," Esperanza said.

"That would be to his credit," Linda answered. "Any man who is a man is my father's enemy. It is only the weak and petty who allow him to manipulate them."

Esperanza looked around in quick fear. "You must take more care of what you say," she warned. "Do you want him to hear you?"

"And what if he does hear me?" Linda challenged. "I've made no secret of how I feel."

"He is your father."

"And you are my mother. Do you think I don't know how he treats you? Do you think I don't long for the day when we can leave this place together?"

"Please," Esperanza said in a frightened voice. "You mustn't say such things."

Linda watched Slocum ride toward the corral for a final inspection of the new horses he had brought down from Texas.

"Someday," she said aloud, "someday a man like *Señor* Slocum will come and take me away from this place."

Slocum looked in toward the horses and saw that they were already being branded with the humpbacked "S" mark Soltano used for his brand. That was all well and good, Slocum thought, but technically, since Soltano hadn't yet paid him for the horses, they weren't his to brand. No matter, it made no difference whether the horses were branded or not. Slocum damn sure didn't intend to let the horses be stolen from him. If he had to, he would take them back, brand and all.

Outside the hacienda, leaning against the fence, watching as the horses were being branded, stood a man named Fidel Nunez. Nunez was the one who had questioned Soltano whether or not Slocum would ride with him.

Nunez had watched Slocum ride in with Pedro and the horses, and had watched him at the well, then followed him to the house. Nunez was a hired hand, and was not permitted inside the house, so he had no idea of what went on while Slocum was inside, but he did see Slocum come back out of the house and he did see that the tall American rode not north, toward Texas, but south, toward Santa Luz.

So, Nunez thought. *Don Soltano was right. Every man does have his price, and he has found Slocum's price.* That was important information to Nunez, because though he worked on Soltano's ranch, he was providing information to the man at whose side he had fought in the guerrilla war, Emiliano Delgado.

A few minutes later, unobserved by anyone at the rancho, Nunez mounted his horse and rode off. He rode away from the hacienda in one direction, but as soon as he was out of sight, he changed course and headed straight for Delgado's ranch to give him the information about the fresh horses and the tall American gunfighter. Delgado would be glad to have such information, though he wouldn't be pleased to hear that Soltano was bringing gunfighters down from the north.

Delgado was a short, stocky man with a curving moustache and chin stubble. For fifteen years he had fought a guerrilla war against the government in Mexico City, until he came to an accommodation with them. He had learned to live in the mountains and villages, and he was leather-tough from his ordeal.

Now Delgado was a landowner. He had become one of the very people he had fought against for such a long time. He had not adapted well to his new station. His house was not a fine, elegant hacienda like Soltano's; it was a shack which barely kept out the weather. He was a man who had learned the logistics of keeping a guerrilla army supplied, but his guerrilla skills had not prepared him for the complexities of running a ranch. It didn't matter, though. He was more concerned with fighting the war against Soltano than with raising cattle.

Delgado knew that he was at a disadvantage. He had a small group of non-fighting peons allied with him, whereas Soltano had a large force of paid professionals. Delgado had neither the men, nor the guns that Soltano could buy with all his gold and silver. But Delgado did have Nunez inside Soltano's operation, and Nunez had just reported to him that Slocum wasn't returning to Texas, but was going to stay in Santa Luz.

"You are sure Soltano has bought this man?" Delgado asked.

"*Sí.* I am very sure."

Delgado stroked his chin stubble and squinted his dark brown eyes.

"Then there is only one thing to do," Delgado said. "We must go to Santa Luz and scare him off."

"Forgive me, *Señor* Delgado," Nunez said. "But this man, John Slocum, does not look like the man one can easily frighten. I do not think we will be able to scare him off."

"If we can't scare him off, we will do something else," Delgado suggested.

"What else can we do?"

"We can kill him," Delgado said simply.

3

Slocum looked at the little town as he rode into it. He'd never been here before, but he had been in a hundred small towns just like Santa Luz, on both sides of the border. It made no difference that this town consisted of adobe buildings laid out around a dusty plaza, baking under the hot Mexican sun. It could have been Laramie or Deadwood, or Hayes or Tombstone. In many ways, they were all alike. They were all the insignificant efforts of man to scratch a mark on the land, leave some monument behind when they turned to ashes and dust.

Slocum dismounted in front of the livery stable, and a gnarled old man came shuffling out from inside. He waved his hand at the flies which were buzzing around his head.

"*Sí, señor?* Do you wish to board your horse?"

"Feed him oats, give him a good rubdown," Slocum said, taking the saddlebag off and draping it across his shoulder. He pulled his Winchester from its sheath, hefted it in a brawny fist. He pointed to the pistols he had taken from the Delgado men who had shadowed him on the trail.

"Do you know any of the men who ride for Delgado?"

"*Sí, señor.*"

"There may be a couple of his men looking for these guns," he said. "I had to take them."

The stableman's eyes grew wide. "You took the guns from Delgado's men?"

"Yes," Slocum answered without elaboration. "Hope they take 'em without trying to make any trouble for anyone. But, if they are interested in raising a little hell, tell 'em I'll be around."

"*Si,*" the liveryman said. He took Slocum's paint and started inside quickly, as if trying to avoid any further involvement.

"Is there a hotel in this town?" Slocum called after him.

"Only one, *señor*. Hotel de Oro," the liveryman said, pointing across the plaza and down the street about a block.

"*Gracias.*"

As Slocum walked across the dusty street to the hotel, he noticed that people seemed to be moving out of his way. The first couple of times, he assumed it was the natural inclination of peasants to avoid any sort of contact, but it wasn't just peasants who reacted that way. The town businessmen also seemed wary of him, standing in the doors of their establishments, then walking quickly back inside as he approached. In the hotel, even the desk clerk seemed hesitant to come near him.

"Room," said Slocum.

"*Sí,*" the clerk answered. He reached up to a line of

hooks on the wall behind him and took down a key, then tossed it to Slocum.

"What's wrong with this town?" Slocum asked.

"*Que?*"

"This town. What's wrong with it? Everywhere I go, people move away from me like I got measles or something. What's going on?"

"It is Don Soltano, *señor.*"

"Soltano? What does he have to do with it?"

"It is known that you are Soltano's man," the clerk explained. "The people are afraid of Soltano. You are his *pistolero,* so they are afraid of you."

Slocum blew the dust off the registration book and signed his name. "So that's what it is, huh?"

"*Sí, señor.*"

"Well, we can get that straightened out in a hurry. I'm not Soltano's man," Slocum said. "I am nobody's man."

"But you brought horses for Don Soltano to ride against Delgado."

"How did you know that?"

"*Señor,* it is known by everyone that you brought the horses down from Texas to be used by Soltano."

"Yes, I did bring some horses to Soltano. But as soon as I'm paid for them, I'm getting out of here," Slocum said. "Anyway, from what I hear there are two parties to this war. What about Delgado? Are the people as afraid of him as they are Soltano?"

"No, *señor.*"

"Why not?"

"Delgado is one of the people. The people do not fear him, they love him."

"Well, good for Delgado. But, like I said, I'm not involved."

Slocum climbed the narrow stairs to the second-floor

room. Once in the room he poured water from a big earthenware pitcher into a basin and rinsed off the trail dust. After that he decided that he needed something for the trail dust in his throat as well. He went back downstairs and walked up the street to the local cantina, Tecolote. The sun had just set, and though it was no longer visible, there was one last, dying flare of red light spread across the western horizon. The heat which had saturated the buildings and the street during the day was now being given back, so there was little relief from the twilight. Slocum wiped beads of sweat from his brow.

Instead of the familiar batwings across the front door, Tecolote's opening was guarded by long strings of multicolored glass beads. Slocum parted them with his hands, then stepped inside as they clacked back together behind him. For a brief moment all conversation stopped and everyone looked toward him. Even the bartender took notice, though he was busily engaged in lighting the lanterns on a wagon wheel which had been lowered from the ceiling. Slocum stood there for a moment, self-conscious about being the center of all attention.

A young, very pretty girl smiled at him. "You are American?"

"Yes."

"I like Americans," she said. "Welcome to the Tecolote." She brushed her hair back from her face, then moved along the bar to stand beside him. The others resumed their private conversations. Slocum heard the names Soltano and Delgado. Though he could speak a smattering of Spanish, the gossip was flowing so thick and fast that he was unable to understand what anyone was actually saying.

The pulley squeaked as the bartender hauled the wagon wheel back up to ceiling, then tied off the rope. The glowing lanterns spread a soft, golden light over the place, dispelling the evening shadows which had come in with the setting of the sun.

"What you want to drink, *señor?*" the bartender asked, wiping his hands on his apron as he moved to stand in front of Slocum.

"*Cerveza,*" Slocum said. "And something for the girl."

"*Gracias,*" the girl said with a pretty smile. She brushed her hair aside again. It was an innocent gesture, an unconscious gesture, and yet the movement tautened the bright-colored fabric of her dress against a well-formed breast.

"My name is Angelina," the girl said. Her brown eyes glowed brightly, her cheeks were dimpled. "Angelina Munoz. You are Juan Slocum."

"John," Slocum corrected.

The girl laughed "*Sí,* John." She scrooched her lips up to form the "Jh" sound.

"How do you know who I am?" Slocum asked.

"Everyone in town knows who you are," Angelina said. "You have come to help Don Soltano."

"Everyone in town is wrong," Slocum said.

The girl looked genuinely confused. "You are not John Slocum?"

"That's who I am, all right. But I'm not here to help Soltano, or anyone else."

"But it is said that Don Soltano is bringing horses and American men down to fight Delgado for him. You are an American. You came with the horses, no?"

"I came with the horses, yes. But as soon as I get the money Soltano owes me, I'm leaving. This isn't my fight and I don't intend to get involved in any of this."

Angelina put her hand on Slocum's arm and smiled again. Her dimples deepened. "Don Soltano is my employer. But I am glad you are not a *pistolero* for him," she said.

"You work for Soltano?"

"*Sí*. I work here, and he owns the Tecolote. Also, he owns the cafe, the livery stable, and the market. He is a very powerful man with much money, and he controls many people, good and bad."

"I can see that," Slocum said. "I just wish he had his money with him now. Or at least enough of it to pay me what he owes me." He drank the last of his drink. "I guess there's nothing to do now but wait."

"If you stay with me, I will make it so you do not mind waiting for your money," Angelina offered. She leaned into him, pressing her thighs and breasts against him. He could feel the heat of her body through the clothes which separated them.

"If I stay with you I may forget what I'm waiting for," Slocum teased. Gently, he pushed her away, rattled the tabletop with coins fished from his pocket, then with a nod of his head by way of saying goodbye, started through the door.

"John Slocum," she called after him. He turned toward her and she smiled seductively. "Will I see you again?"

"You might. I'm staying at the hotel. Do you ever come there?"

Angelina smiled broadly. "*Sí*. My mother and father own the hotel."

"If they own the hotel, why do you work here?"

"Because it is more exciting to work in a cantina than in a hotel," Angelina said.

Slocum smiled back at her. "Sometimes there is too much excitement in a place like this," he suggested. He nodded at her again, then pushed through the beaded doorway and went back outside. The sun was completely down now and the street was very dark. There were no lanterns on posts in this small town, and only the moon and a few dim squares of light, splashing through open windows, kept the street from being as black as the inside of a pit.

Slocum felt them before he heard them, and he heard them before he saw them. Two men with knives jumped from the dark shadows between the buildings, and only that innate sense which allowed him to perceive danger when there was no other sign saved his life. He was moving out of the way of the attack at the exact moment the two men were starting it, so that their knives, swinging in low, vicious arcs, did not immediately disembowel him.

Despite the quickness of his reaction, one of the knives struck him, and as Slocum went down to the street, rolling to get away from them, the flashing blade opened a deep wound in his side. The knife was so sharp and wielded so adroitly that Slocum barely felt it. He knew, however, that the assassins had drawn blood.

For all their skill with the blades, the assassins had made a big mistake. Both of them were wearing white peon shirts and trousers, so that despite the darkness of the street they were easy to see. One of the assassins moved quickly to finish Slocum off before he could recover, and that was the attacker's mistake. Slocum twisted around on the ground, then thrust his feet out, catching the Mexican in the chest, driving him back several feet. The other one moved in, keeping Slocum off his feet, keeping him away from his gun.

The assailants were good: skilled and agile. But they were small, giving Slocum a little advantage, though his size was nearly overcome by their quickness. Slocum sent a booted foot whistling toward one of them, catching the man in the groin. Then he lunged upward, and rammed stiff fingers that gouged the other in both eyes.

"Aiiyeee!" the assailant screamed, dropping his knife and reaching up to his face.

The one who had been kicked in the groin reached his partner and, pulling on him, broke off the fight. They skittered around the corner of the building and for a brief moment Slocum got a good view of both their faces in the light which spilled from the open adobe window of the cantina. He fixed the memory of them in his mind. If he ran across those two again, he would know them.

Slocum felt the nausea rise up in him. Bile surged in his throat. Dizzy, he went back into the cantina. Once again all conversation stopped at his entrance, and this time the silence lingered like a leaden weight over Slocum's head. Everyone stared at him. When he had come in earlier, they had stared at him with curiosity. This time their mouths opened in shock.

Slocum didn't realize it, but he was quite an apparition to behold. He stood there in the beaded doorway, ashen-faced, holding his hand over a wound which spilled bright-red blood between his fingers. He surveyed the room for just a moment, then, with effort, walked to the bar.

"*Tequila,*" he ordered. The solemn-faced bartender poured him a glass and Slocum took it, then turned around to face the silent patrons. By now his side was drenched with blood from his wound, and the blood was beginning to soak into the dark earth of the floor.

"John!" Angelina said, moving to him quickly. Slocum held out his hand to keep her away.

"If any of you had anything to do with me getting knifed, I'm going to give you fair warning. The next man who even looks at me cross-eyed, I'm going to blow his head off." Slocum looked at them, tossed down the drink, and set it on the bar. Then he walked calmly from the cantina. He was dizzy and lightheaded from the loss of blood, and he reached out to grab the door frame and steady himself as he walked through the door.

Slocum started back to his hotel once more, only this time he stayed far enough away from the buildings so that there was no chance of anyone jumping him from the shadows again. He moved out into the middle of the street and lurched along with a stumbling, staggering gait, trying to stay on his feet, though his head was now spinning so badly he could scarcely stand.

When he finally reached the front of the hotel he fell against the door, managed to keep his feet, then stumbled through. He knew he had to get off his feet quickly, so he lurched toward the stairs to keep from falling on the floor.

"Señor?" the desk clerk said, startled by Slocum's unusual entry. *"Señor,* are you hurt?"

"No," Slocum said. "I'm fine. I'm just fine."

Slocum leaned against the wall beside the stairs for a moment to get his breath, and when he did so, he left a stain of his blood on the wall. Then, holding his side, Slocum climbed the stairs to his room. Once inside he ripped the bed sheet in two and wrapped it around his side, pressing it tightly against his wound. When the crude bandage was in place, he fell across the bed, closed his eyes, and passed out cold.

4

When the tall American staggered away from the cantina, Angelina went back inside to return to her work. She smiled at the customers and served them drinks, and once, when Montoya played his guitar, she did a little dance for them. But her mind wasn't on her work. Her mind was on the man named John Slocum.

"I did not believe the Alverez brothers would let the *gringo* live," a man at one of the tables said. "They've never failed before."

"The *gringo* is a big, powerful man," one of the others at the table replied. "And they say he is faster than lightning with his guns."

"But he didn't use his guns. They used the knives, and he fought them with his bare hands."

"He will be a hard one for Delgado to kill."

"If just one of Soltano's *gringos* is so powerful, what will it be when all of his *gringos* arrive?"

"Delgado will not be able to defeat such men."

"You are mistaken. The tall American is not fighting for Soltano," Angelina offered. It was a rather shocking thing for Angelina to speak out so, because as a serving girl she was not allowed to join in any conversation unless it be to tease a customer into buying more drinks . . . or her own services. She was expected to keep quiet in affairs of business, especially when men were discussing something as serious as a range war.

"What did you say?" one of the men asked.

Angelina put her hand to her lips. She hadn't meant to actually say anything, the words had just popped out of her mouth, and now it was too late. She looked down toward the floor and her cheeks flamed in embarrassment.

"I'm sorry," she apologized. "I spoke out of turn."

"No. You were talking to the *gringo*. What do you know about him?"

"I know nothing about him," Angelina answered. "Only that he said he isn't here to fight for Soltano."

"Maybe we are wrong," one of the men said. "Maybe he isn't here to fight for Soltano."

"Yes. If he would fight for Soltano, does it not make sense that he would stay at Soltano's hacienda? The hacienda is a fine place to stay. Here there is nothing. Even the hotel is nothing."

"Of course he is fighting for Soltano," the first man insisted. "Did he not bring fine horses? And were we not told that Soltano would be hiring *gringos* who were very fast with the gun?"

"We do not know that he is fast with the gun. No one has seen him use his gun."

"You can see by his eyes. You do not have to see a rattlesnake strike to know it is dangerous. He is a *pis-*

tolero, and he is employed by Soltano."

"But he told the girl he was not."

"The girl is a whore. The words a man says to a whore mean nothing."

"Yes, many times I have told a *puta* 'I love you,'" one of the men said, as he smacked his lips as if in a kiss.

Everyone within earshot laughed at that comment, and Angelina, her cheeks burning even more than before, walked away from them and busied herself by picking up empty glasses from the tables and bar and taking them to the kitchen.

A few moments later the bartender came back to the kitchen and saw Angelina washing dishes.

"Why are you in here?" he asked. "The customers cannot buy drinks from you if you are in the kitchen."

Angelina wiped her eyes. "I am no good to you tonight, Julio," she said. "The men laugh at me, so they will not wish to buy drinks from me."

"You shouldn't have spoken as you did," Julio said. "It is not a woman's place to speak about such things."

"I know I should not have spoken, but I am frightened for the American," Angelina explained. "Everyone believes he is a *pistolero* for Soltano. I fear someone will kill him."

Julio laughed. "Someone already tried, but you see what they got for their troubles. Do not concern yourself for the *gringo.* I think he can take care of himself. Now, dry your eyes and leave the kitchen work for Maria. She is fat and ugly and no one would wish to buy drinks from her. You are young and beautiful. Go back out front where you belong."

Angelina smiled through her tears and wiped her eyes. "I will sell drinks," she said. "But tonight no man can buy my favors. Tonight I am going to see the *gringo* and tend to his wounds."

When Angelina got off work later that night she hurried through the dark street to the hotel. In the kitchen of her parents' hotel she found a jar of salve and a tin of crushed aloe leaves. She also sneaked a spare key to Slocum's room, then, armed with a bar of soap, some fresh wrappings for bandages, salve, and the medicinal herbs, she sneaked by the sleeping desk clerk, climbed the stairs slowly and quietly, and let herself into Slocum's room.

The room was hot and sticky, and she could smell the blood from his wound. She felt around in the dark until she found the bedside table and candle. A moment later she found the box of lucifers and struck one, then held the flame to the candle until a small light perched atop the taper. The dark of the room was pushed away.

Because of the wound, Slocum was sleeping much deeper than normally. He didn't hear Angelina when she came into his room, nor did he awaken when she lit the candle. It was only when she sat on the bed beside him that his eyes snapped open. Even then, he awoke more from curiosity than from a sense of danger.

"What?" Slocum asked. "What are you doing?"

"Shh," Angelina whispered. She began unwinding the sheet from around his side. "I'm going to treat your wound," she said.

"It'll be all right."

"No. It must be cleaned and treated," she said. "I have soap and medicines."

"Why do you want to do this? I thought this town wanted me dead."

"The men who attacked you are the Alverez brothers. They work for Delgado," Angelina said. "They are very bad men. Do not blame everyone who lives here for what the Alverez brothers have done." She had the bandage unwound now, and she sucked in her breath as she looked at the blood which had coagulated around the wound. "You have bled much," she said. "You are lucky you did not die."

"Why would Delgado want to kill me?" Slocum asked. "I don't even know the man."

"Maybe he thinks you work for Soltano."

"Yes. Everyone seems to think that. Well, I don't. I'm just waiting for the money he owes me, then I'll be on my way. I don't buy into trouble, especially in a foreign country."

"You must be still now," Angelina said as she poured water from the porcelain pitcher into the basin. "I will clean your wound, then dress it."

Slocum lay back down and folded his hands behind his head. The muscles in his arms, shoulders, and chest rippled as he did so, and he looked up at the beautiful young woman who brought the water to the small table, then sat again on the bed beside him.

"All right," he said.

Gently, Angelina began cleaning the blood from Slocum's side. The cut started just above the beltline, then disappeared below the waistband of his pants. Angelina unbuttoned his trousers, then slipped them down. The hair which began as a tiny dark line at his navel broadened into a dark, curling bush. She stopped there before any more was revealed.

"It is not deep," she said. "There is nothing bad cut. It only bleeds a lot."

Slocum looked directly into her eyes, saw the latent smoke of lust in their depths.

For reasons she couldn't explain, Angelina felt a tre-

mendous heat suffusing her body as she cleaned him.
She was a prostitute, a woman who had seen many naked
men. And yet here, in the innocence of this room, the
situation seemed different. As if mesmerized, she slowly
pulled Slocum's trousers a little farther down, though not
all the way. It was almost as if she were a young, virgin
girl, seeing a man for the first time, and she sucked air
audibly through her teeth.

"You . . . you are a handsome man, John Slocum," she
said quietly.

Angelina felt Slocum's abdomen. It was incredibly
hot, perhaps fevered by the wound, and yet she could
feel the pulsing of his blood just beneath the skin. Though
it wasn't necessary for her to pull his trousers the rest of
the way down, she did. As she bathed him, she bent
over and the top of her blouse fell forward, exposing the
curve of her breasts. She felt a heat there, then looked
up to see that Slocum was looking at the view she had
presented him. She smiled, almost shyly, and continued
to work.

When his wound was completely clean she applied a
salve to it, then rubbed on the crushed medicinal herbs.
"Does it feel good?" she asked.

"Yeah," Slocum croaked.

Angelina finished applying the medication but she let
her hand continue to rub his skin. Her hand moved in
ever-widening circles until finally she reached his penis.
She squeezed it, felt it begin to grow in her hands. She
smiled down at him.

"I think maybe I should take care of this too," she
said.

"I think that would be a good idea," Slocum said
huskily.

Angelina peeled out of her blouse, then stepped out

of her skirt. She stood in the candlelight beside the bed, displaying her young, beautiful body to him. The tautened nipples glowed in the light, while shadows kept mysterious the promise of her thighs. She sat back on the bed and looked at him.

"But you are wounded," she said. "Perhaps you cannot make love while you are wounded."

"We'll find a way," Slocum said.

"Yes. We'll find a way," Angelina agreed. She leaned down and kissed his neck, then started working her way down his chest. Slocum could feel the soft, velvet heat of her darting tongue as she licked his skin, trailing back and forth until she stopped at his nipple and flicked her tongue over it several times.

Slocum tried to move over her, but the pain stabbed at him. When Angelina saw that, she smiled gently, put her cool fingers on his shoulders to indicate that he should stay where he was, then moved over him, straddling him and taking him into her, orchestrating the moment for both of them.

Slocum felt Angelina over him, pressing down against his thrusts, making love to him. He felt her jerk in wild spasms as the jolts of rapture racked her body. With a groan, she fell across him, even as he was spending himself in her in his final, convulsive shudders.

They lay that way for several moments with Angelina on top, allowing the pleasure to drain from her body slowly. Finally she got up and looked down at him. She licked her lips and they glowed in the gleam of candlelight.

"I am a prostitute," she said. "I have done this many times, with many men. But never before have I done it because I wanted to."

"And you wanted to with me?"

"Yes."

"Why?"

"I . . . I don't know why," Angelina said. She reached down and touched his organ. It was slack now, spent of the energy which had lifted it moments earlier. "Never before have I felt what I felt with you, John Slocum." She looked at the cut, saw that their lovemaking had opened it up a little. "Oh," she said. "I'm sorry, I have made it hurt more."

Slocum chuckled. "Believe me, it was worth it."

"I will clean the wound again, and this time I will bandage it."

Slocum put his hand on Angelina's naked thigh. "Don't bandage everything," he teased. "I might have use for it again."

Angelina smiled. "You are quite a man, John Slocum," she said.

She didn't leave Slocum's room until just before dawn.

5

The noise in his head sounded like the inside of a drum. Slocum opened his eyes and looked around him. The room was lighted by the spill of early morning sunlight. The smell of Angelina's musky perfume hung in the still morning air, but she was gone.

The drum sounded again, a pounding on the door.

"Yeah," Slocum said. "Yeah, just a minute." He sat up and ran his hand through his raven-dark hair. He was stiff and sore.

More pounding. He shook off the sleepiness, struggled to clear the cobwebs from his brain. Groggily, Slocum got out of bed, then staggered over to the door and jerked it open.

"What the hell is it?" he growled.

"*Señor* Slocum?" A young, well-dressed man was standing just on the other side of the door, holding an envelope in his hand. "You are *Señor* Slocum, are you not?"

"Who are you?" Slocum asked without answering the young man's question.

"My name is Joaquin Soltano."

"Joaquin Soltano? A relative of Don Soltano?"

"*Sí*. I am his son."

Slocum smiled. "Well, that's more like it," he said. "You got my money?"

"Money?"

"Yes, my money . . . the money your father owes me for the purebreds."

"I am sorry, *señor*, I know nothing about any money," the young Soltano said.

"You mean your father didn't send you here to pay me?"

"No, *señor*."

Slocum swore. "Well, damn it, boy, if he sent you for anything else, I'm not interested. I already told him, just like I told everyone in this flytrap village, I have no intention of riding for Don Soltano."

Slocum started to close the door, but Joaquin reached for it.

"Please, *senōr*, I am my father's son, that is true. But I am not here for my father."

"Who are you here for?"

Joaquin held up the envelope. "I am here for my sister. You met her yesterday. Do you remember her?"

Slocum remembered the beautiful young woman he had met at Solanto's hacienda the day before. For the time being last night, Angelina had managed to push Linda out of his mind, but at the mention of her, it all came back to him . . . the soft fire eyes, the high sheen of her black hair, the light olive skin.

"Yeah, I remember her," he answered.

"Please, *Señor* Slocum, may I come in?"

Slocum stepped away from the door by way of invitation. "Why didn't I meet you yesterday?" he asked.

"I arrived late last night from Mexico City," Joaquin said.

"Mexico City? Then you must've brought my money." Slocum took the envelope from the boy and shook it. It seemed too thin to contain cash, though it could contain a bank draft. He looked at it more closely, then saw Linda's initials in the sealing wax.

"I'm sorry, *señor*. I told you. It is not money," Joaquin repeated.

Slocum opened the envelope and pulled out a sheet of stationery. It was very expensive, and the writing was in bold, elegant strokes. It was also in Spanish, and Slocum couldn't read Spanish. He held it out toward Joaquin.

"What does it say?" he asked.

"My sister says she will bring a buggy by later on. And a basket of food," Joaquin said, reading quickly. "She will show you some of the country."

"What about the money that's owed to me?"

"I'm afraid I do not know."

"But you must've brought it from Mexico City."

"I did bring a satchel to my father from Mexico City. I do not know what it contained."

Slocum rubbed his chin as he looked at the youth. He was about twenty or so, Slocum figured, and he wore a pearl-handled Smith & Wesson.

"I hope there was money in that satchel," Slocum said. As Slocum dressed in front of the young man, he winced in pain once. That was when Joaquin saw his bandaged side.

"What is that?" Joaquin asked, pointing to the wound.

"That, *amigo*, is a calling card from Delgado, by way of the Alverez brothers," Slocum replied. "It seems they don't want me throwing in with your father."

"You are very lucky, *Señor* Slocum," Joaquin said. "I know the Alverez brothers. They are evil men who do not normally warn a person. They kill quickly and silently."

"Yes, well, I think these boys had that very idea in mind," Slocum agreed, smiling faintly.

"And you drove them away?" Joaquin was obviously impressed.

"Like you say, I was lucky."

"Perhaps my father hopes to buy your luck as well as your gun."

"Look," Slocum said sharply, "I'm getting damned tired of telling everyone that I'm not working for your father. I didn't come down here to work for him, and I don't intend to work for him. If he sent you out here to talk me into it, you can just go back and tell him to go straight to hell. All I want is the money due me."

"You mean you won't work for my father?"

"No," Slocum said resolutely.

Inexplicably, Joaquin smiled broadly, then reached out and shook Slocum's hand. "Good! I am very glad. It could be, *Señor* Slocum, that I have misjudged you. I should have known better. I should have listened to my sister. She is a much better judge of a person than I am."

Slocum looked at Joaquin in surprise. "Maybe I've misjudged you as well," Slocum said, puzzled by Joaquin's strange reaction. "You don't seem all that upset that I'm not working for your father."

"*Señor* Slocum, I am my father's son, and therefore I must obey him," Joaquin explained. "But, like my sister, I do not like him very much."

"From what I gather, no one does," Slocum said.

"I will tell my sister I delivered the message for her," Joaquin said. He smiled broadly. "My sister is a beautiful woman, no?"

"Your sister is a beautiful woman—yes," Slocum answered back.

Joaquin smiled again. "She likes you, *Señor* Slocum. I do not know why this is so, but she likes you." Joaquin touched the brim of his sombrero, then made his departure.

After the boy left, Slocum finished dressing, buckling his belt gingerly over the wound, which was more painful than it had been the night before. The cut ran beneath his belt, and he had to make a pad out of a piece of a bed sheet to keep the belt from hurting more. When he was fully dressed and padded, he stood in front of the mirror and drew his gun. He winced with pain as he jerked it from his holster, but he didn't lose any speed. Certainly if his life depended on getting the gun out quickly enough, the pain would have no effect on his draw. He slipped the pistol back into his holster, then left his room.

As Slocum started down the stairs he realized that he was famished, and with reason. He hadn't eaten since breakfast the day before. He stepped out into the morning sun and squinted at the buildings until he saw a cafe. He crossed the street and went inside.

The cafe smelled of chili peppers, garlic, onion, fried beef, and coffee.

"Do you want something to eat?" The woman who asked the question seemed friendly. If the word was out against him, it either hadn't reached this woman or, if it had, she didn't care.

"Maybe half a dozen eggs and..."

"I'm sorry, *señor,* no eggs," the woman apologized.

"What do you have?"

"Chili, tamales, beans, tortillas, beefsteak," the woman said.

"Beans, beefsteak, tortillas," Slocum ordered. "Do you have coffee?"

"*Sí.* I make very good coffee."

"Good, good. I'd like a cup, and keep it filled, will you?"

"*Sí,*" the woman answered. She used her apron as a heat pad and brought the big, blue coffeepot right to his table. She poured Slocum a cup before she went back to the kitchen to fix his breakfast.

Five minutes later Slocum had the fare before him, and he ate heartily, washing it down with a third cup of coffee.

After he finished and while he was paying his bill, he heard shouts of excitement out on the street.

"What is that?" he asked.

"I do not know, *señor,*" the woman answered, giving him his change.

Slocum put the change in his pocket, then stepped out into the plaza. A crowd was gathering quickly, and more people surged past him, hurrying for the center of the town square. Curious, Slocum followed in their wake.

In the center of the street two burros loped toward him, shying from left to right as the townspeople tried unsuccessfully to catch them. A body was draped across each burro, belly down. Neither of the bodies were wearing sandals, and their feet looked still and cold in death.

Slocum ran out into the square and caught the first burro. He blocked the second one from going past him. Two men came up then to capture the second. A jabber of excited talk flowed around him, but they were all speaking Spanish, and they were talking so fast that he couldn't understand what they were saying. He got the feeling, however, that they were making some sort of accusation toward him.

Slocum unraveled the cheap manila rope from around the dead man on the burro he had stopped, then turned him over. He drew in a sharp breath and recoiled in horror. The man wasn't just dead, he was mutilated. His eyes had been gouged out and there was a hole in his chest where the heart used to be. His crotch was a bloody gash—stuffed in his mouth were his testicles. It was a particularly gruesome sight, even to someone who had stared death in the face as often as Slocum had.

Slocum turned away and closed his eyes. For a moment he was afraid he was going to lose his breakfast, but he fought against the urge. Then, when he had himself under control, he forced himself to look at the other corpse. It was mutilated in the same way as the first, but this time he was prepared for it.

There was something familiar about the bodies, and Slocum studied their faces for a moment. Their eyes were gone, their features badly distorted, but finally Slocum recognized the men. They were the two who jumped him the night before, the Alverez brothers. Now he realized what the crowd was talking about, and he looked up at them. He could see the accusing glances in the faces of the people who surrounded him. They thought he had killed and mutilated the two brothers.

"I had nothing to do with this," he told the crowd. *"Nada."*

"You fought these men last night, *señor,*" one of the men in the crowd said.

"Yeah, and if I could've gotten to my gun in time, I

would have killed them last night. But even if I killed them, I wouldn't have cut them up like this. I'm not a butcher."

Beyond those who were crowding close to him, menacing him with sheer numbers and angry faces, Slocum saw Angelina gesturing to him. All around her, the crowd continued to press forward.

Slocum's hands dropped to the butts of his pistols. The crowd, seeing that action, hesitated.

"First one gets close enough for me to smell gets a lead ball in the gullet," Slocum warned. The crowd backed off, and Slocum pushed through them to find Angelina. She was gone, but when he returned to his hotel a few minutes later, she surprised him in the upstairs hall.

"Angelina," he said, "listen. You know I didn't kill those men. You were with me last night. And if I had, I wouldn't have mutilated the corpses like that."

"I know that is true, John Slocum."

"I want you to tell the townspeople I had nothing to do with it."

"They also know you did not do this," Angelina said breathlessly. "Soltano did it. But it is very dangerous for you now, because they believe you had Soltano do it for you."

"Soltano did that?"

Angelina nodded.

"Why? How did he . . . ?"

"They are Delgado's men. They tried to kill you last night."

Suddenly it dawned on Slocum that there really was some connection with the fact that the Alverez brothers had tried to kill him last night. Soltano had the brothers killed for attacking Slocum, knowing the townspeople would make the connection. Slocum didn't like that. He didn't like that at all. It put him in a peculiar, and unpleasant, position.

Slocum wanted to question Angelina more, but before he could, she was gone, whisking down the stairs as if her life depended on it. Slocum ran down the stairs after her, but by the time he reached the street she was gone. He stood in front of the hotel and looked up and down the street both ways, puzzled as to what could have happened to her.

"Good morning, *Señor* Slocum," a voice said. The voice was soft, and musical, like the chiming of windbells.

Slocum looked toward the voice and saw a sulky parked in front of the hotel. Linda Soltano sat holding the reins of a beautiful matched pair of white horses. An old woman was sitting in a jump seat which jutted from the rear of the sulky. It was the same old woman Slocum had seen at the well the day before.

"My brother told me he delivered my letter," Linda said.

"Yes," Slocum answered. "Yes, he did." He had run down here in pursuit of Angelina. Now that woman completely slipped his mind. He could see only the beauty of this creature who was in front of him.

"This is *Señora* Filomena Calderon," Linda said, introducing the old woman. The old woman reeked of strong spirits and crushed mint used to hide the aroma of her breath. "She will be our chaperone."

"Chaperone?"

"But of course, *Señor* Slocum. You did not expect that a young lady of my standing would go on a buggy ride with you alone, did you?" Linda asked, as if shocked at such a suggestion.

"No, I guess not."

"Then, shall we go?"

"Yes," Slocum said. He climbed onto the seat beside Linda and she slapped the reins against the back of the team. Slocum could feel the heat of her thigh against him, and he knew that there was enough room on the seat for them to sit a little farther apart. He made no effort to move, however, and neither did she. He considered that a good sign.

6

As Slocum and Linda passed through the town plaza, the people of the village stepped back to give them plenty of room. Some of them even turned their backs as the carriage passed.

"Why do they do that?" Slocum asked.

"They are afraid of my father," Linda answered matter-of-factly. "And because they fear him, they also fear me. Not a very pleasant legacy to inherit from one's father, is it?"

Slocum didn't know what to say. In fact, Linda seemed as ill-at-ease with the people as they did with her, and she stared straight ahead. Finally they were beyond the edge of town and the tension eased. Even the team seemed to sense it as they broke into a spirited trot. The buggy rolled along briskly for several minutes, putting some distance between them and the town.

Linda drove to a grassy canyon which was profusely

dotted with wildflowers of every type and hue. It was a phenomenal contrast to the rocks and cactus which had been so much of the scenery since Slocum arrived in Mexico. Slocum mentioned this.

"Yes, it is beautiful here," Linda agreed. "It seems to make the rest of life so much harsher, knowing that such beauty is close by."

Slocum chuckled. "Your life doesn't seem that harsh to me. Hacienda del Soltano looks like a castle."

"Yes, I will confess, my prison is a beautiful one," Linda said.

"Your prison? Why do you call it your prison?"

Linda held her finger to her lips and looked over at Filomena. The chaperone was sound asleep, snoring softly.

"We will discuss this later," she said. She smiled. "First, we eat. Are you hungry? I brought a very nice lunch for us."

In truth, Slocum wasn't hungry, thanks to the large breakfast he had eaten that morning. But many years on the trail had taught him the trick of eating and drinking his fill when it was available, because there were so many times when it wouldn't be available. And though his appetite might not be stimulated by hunger, it could certainly be stimulated by the company he was with.

"I'm starved," he lied.

"I am glad. I would hate to waste good food on someone who has no appetite."

Linda unfolded a wet burlap bag and took out a bottle of wine. By wrapping the bottle in the bag, the wine was cold when the water evaporated. As a result, it was as cold as if it had been kept in an icy mountain stream. She handed the bottle to Slocum.

"If you'll open the bottle, I'll set out the food," she

said. "We can use that flat rock as our table."

Linda spread a red, green, and white checkered tablecloth, then began setting out the food—cold chicken, roast beef, beans, pickled cucumbers, and freshly baked bread. There were two glasses in the basket, and Slocum filled the glasses with the deep red, cold wine. He gave a glass to Linda.

"Thank you," she said, holding the glass out toward him in a toast. "To friends across the border," she proposed.

"I'll drink to that," Slocum agreed as they touched the glasses together, then drank. The wine was excellent and reminded Slocum of wine he had drunk in some of the finest establishments in San Francisco.

Having toasted, they ate the picnic lunch together. After the meal Slocum poured them each another glass of wine. He noticed that there was only about a third of the bottle left.

"Shouldn't we be saving some wine for the chaperone?" he asked, indicating the sleeping old lady.

"I think the old woman has had enough spirits without having to drink any of ours," Linda said. She giggled and covered her mouth with her hand. "I shouldn't speak of her like that. Filomena is really quite a wonderful person, and if she drinks too much, who is to blame her? She is a gentle lady with a gentle past. She cannot understand what is happening."

"Do you mean the range war between your father and Delgado?"

"Yes," Linda said. "But not just that. My father is . . ." She sighed. "I do not like to speak of my own blood in such a way, but my father is a very cruel and unjust man."

"He's a powerful man," Slocum said. "Sometimes men with great power must do things that seem cruel and unjust."

"I suppose so," Linda said. "But that isn't justification for my father beating my mother, is it?"

"No," Slocum admitted. He didn't like conversations like this, but he was in this one now and there was no decent way he could back off from it. "No, I guess not."

"He beats her, Señor Slocum, not only physically, but ... how do you say it? ... with words as well. The physical beating, I think my mother could stand. The beating with words makes her want to die, and it is for this that I can never forgive my father."

"You're a big girl. Why do you stay with him?" Slocum asked.

"Ah," Linda said, and she smiled. "You have brought up a good point. Why do I stay with him? Because never before have I seen a way to escape from him. Everyone I have ever known has been afraid of my father. He is, as you say, a powerful man. Is it any wonder that people fear him?"

"I guess not," Slocum agreed.

Linda finished her wine, then ran her finger around the rim of the glass. She looked at Slocum with eyes so deep and so dark that Slocum felt he could get lost in them. "Except you," she finally added. "You aren't afraid of him, are you?"

"Afraid of him? No, I can't say that I am," Slocum replied.

Linda smiled. "I knew it. I knew you would be the one who could help me."

"Help you? Help you do what?"

"Help me get away from this place," Linda said. "You

can help me escape from my father."

"Oh, now, wait a minute," Slocum protested, holding his hand out as if warding her away. "You've got the wrong man. I don't want to get involved in anything like that."

"Please, John Slocum. You yourself asked why I don't leave his house. I haven't left because I am afraid. But I wouldn't be afraid with you. You could take Joaquin and me away from here. You could take us across the border to the United States. We would be safe there."

"What about your mother? Would she be coming as well?"

"No," Linda said. "My mother will never leave. She will stay and endure his tyranny."

"You would leave her?"

"I do not want to," Linda admitted. "I have tried many times to talk her into leaving with Joaquin and me. But she will not go. Now the time has come when Joaquin and I must act to save ourselves."

"I see. And you thought the wine, the food, and an afternoon with a pretty girl would make me help you?"

"Yes," Linda admitted. She pulled her knee up under her chin and as she did so, her dress fell back to expose a flash of white thigh. "And if it doesn't, I'm prepared to go as far as I have to to convince you to help us."

"Linda, you don't need to do that. Anyway, I'm not so sure it would be a good idea for you to leave right now. Especially if your mother won't go with you," Slocum said.

"But I must escape, don't you understand?" Linda insisted. "I don't want to be around when my father attacks the Delgado ranch. When that happens, I fear my father's cruelty will know no bounds. You cannot imagine the things my father is capable of doing."

"Maybe I can," Slocum said. "Maybe I've seen some of it."

"What do you mean? When? Where?"

"This morning there were two men killed . . . the Alverez brothers. I understand they worked for Delgado. Do you know anything about it?"

"No," Linda said. "I don't. But if they rode for Delgado, I wouldn't put it past my father to have something to do with their deaths. Wait a minute . . . this morning, you say?"

"Yes. They were murdered, then mutilated and tied to their burros. They came into town belly down."

"Someone came to the hacienda last night after my brother arrived from Mexico City," Linda said. "I heard some whispered conversation, but I couldn't understand what they were talking about. Then, this morning, Pedro was gone, and when he returned, he had blood on his hands. I heard someone ask him about it, and he said he had killed and skinned a coyote."

"A couple of two-legged coyotes, unless I miss my guess," Slocum said. He sighed. "I guess I'm the cause of it."

"You? Why? You did not kill them, did you?"

"No. But your father wants me to come to work for him. Last night those two thought I had already gone to work for Don Soltano. They attacked me with knives, but I drove them off. I believe your father had them killed to force me to work for him."

"You may be right," Linda said. "My father is capable of such cruelty. He is as evil as my mother is good. I am thankful that my brother takes after my mother and not my father."

"By the way, your brother told me he brought a satchel

with him from Mexico City. Was that my money?"

"Yes."

"Then your father can pay me."

"Yes, he can pay you," Linda said. "But he won't."

"What do you mean, he won't?"

"He won't pay you. He still wants your guns, and he thinks he can force you into riding for him by holding back your money."

"Is that so? Well, I intend to pay a call on Don Soltano. I've had about enough of this."

"Please, if you call on my father, be careful."

"Who are you worried about? Your father or me?"

"You," Linda said. "Only you."

Slocum looked off toward the distant horizon, saw a dust devil spring up, scoot along for a short distance, then break apart.

"What about the people your father has hired to ride for him? The Americans. Do you know any of them?"

"I know only that they are all very bad men," she said with a shudder. "I don't know any of them."

"I think I'd better get my money before they arrive. If I don't, I might wind up having to fight the whole lot of them."

"I beg of you, John Slocum, if you get your money, take my brother and me with you."

"Where would I take you?"

"I have an uncle, my father's brother, who lives in Laredo. You could take us there."

Slocum sighed, a long, audible sigh. "All right," he finally relented. "I'll take you there if I can."

"Oh, thank you!" Linda threw her arms around Slocum and, to his surprise, kissed him full on the lips.

Linda pressed herself against him, pushing the big man back on the soft carpet of grass. She lay on top of him, then moved to his mouth with lips which were like fire and ice, turning him to mescal pulp when she kissed him.

"I told you I would take you," he said. "You don't need to do this."

"I'm doing this because I want to," Linda said.

"Filomena?" Slocum cautioned.

"She can sleep through a thunderstorm," Linda went on, and her fingers began pulling at the buttons of her own blouse. A moment later she had bared her breasts, and she took his hands and cupped them around the hot globes of flesh. "I want you, John Slocum," she whispered into his ear. Her breath was hot on his cheek and neck. "I want you to make love to me."

Slocum had no protests remaining, nor did he want to protest any more. He moved his lips to her nipples, then, with his other hand, raised the hem of her dress and was surprised to feel naked thighs under the skirt. He moved his hands up her legs, encountered a tiny bit of silk, then slipped his fingers beneath the silk to feel the moist, hot mound.

"Yes," Linda said in a whimpering voice, moving onto her back and pulling her skirt up. She raised her hips and began pushing down on the silk undergarment, freeing herself.

John unbuttoned his trousers and started to slip them down as he positioned himself between her straining legs. Her rich, sexual scent drifted up to him, inflaming his senses, making him wild with desire. His erection was straining so hard against his trousers that it hurt him.

"Linda?" the duenna called, awakening suddenly. With a quick flurry, John rolled on one side, while Linda sat up and pushed her dress back down. John sat with his back to the sulky as he began to rebutton his pants.

"Yes," Linda answered. "We're over here." Without being seen, Linda slid her hand over and dropped it on Slocum's lap, and then squeezed.

"Don't do that," Slocum cautioned. "It's not pleasant when there's nothing I can do about it."

"You think it is any more pleasant for me?" Linda teased. "I have such a heat about me I feel as if I'm going to catch on fire."

"Then don't make it any worse," Slocum said, taking her hand and moving it gently away.

Filomena got out of the sulky and walked unsteadily toward the two young people.

"Oh," she said. "Have you eaten already? I must have dozed off."

"Don't worry," Linda said. "There is plenty for you." She picked up the wine bottle. "We even saved you some wine."

"Wine? Oh, dear me, I don't know," Filomena said. "I don't drink spirits, you know."

"Yes, I know," Linda answered with a smile and a wink at Slocum. "But perhaps a little wine with your lunch will be all right."

"Yes, I suppose a little wouldn't hurt me," Filomena agreed. She held out a glass and when Linda stopped after pouring the glass half full, Filomena nudged the glass toward her, indicating she should fill it all the way.

"There," Linda said, filling the glass the rest of the way. "Enjoy."

"Did you two young people have a nice conversation?" Filomena asked.

"Yes, very nice," Linda said, looking over at Slocum and smiling broadly, her eyes flashing with the secret they shared. "We had a most interesting conversation." Linda got up then and walked back to the sulky. When

Slocum's erection subsided to the point that he could get up without it being obvious, he walked over to the sulky to join her.

"I'm sorry. I didn't think she would wake up," Linda apologized, but the light in her eyes indicated that she had actually enjoyed the modicum of danger the situation afforded.

"I'm glad it was then instead of five minutes later," Slocum said.

Linda laughed. "She would have had quite a surprise."

Slocum laughed too. He appreciated Linda's sense of daring, and found her all the more intriguing because of it.

"Will you be in your hotel room tonight?" she asked.

"Yes, why?"

"I'll come to see you if I can sneak away," Linda promised.

7

Slocum took a bath late that afternoon, examined his wound and saw that it wasn't puffed or discolored, then put on a fresh bandage. Afterward, he walked down to the cantina for a drink. He skipped supper, not only because he had eaten two big meals already, but also because he was beginning to run short of money. He had expected to turn a good profit from his delivery of the horses, then go back to Texas flush. He had invested heavily in the horses, not only in the time he put in, but also in his own personal funds. It seemed a risk worth taking, but it had not gone as planned. He didn't get the money on delivery, and he was beginning to wonder if he would ever get it at all. He was either going to have to take the horses back or wait a little longer for his money. In either case, he was so short of funds that life was going to be difficult.

He thought about getting into a card game. Perhaps

a little cautious playing could give him a slight cushion. A skilled card player, if he played carefully, without daring, he knew he could improve his fortunes slightly. Though such playing wasn't likely to win any great sum of money, it would provide him with enough to extend the time he could wait.

Slocum allowed himself one drink at the bar, then lit one of his few remaining cheroots. He sat in for a few hands in the card game that was going on in the back of the cantina. One of the other players, he learned from Angelina, was Luis Ortiz. Ortiz was a powerfully built man who wore a bandolier of ammunition across one shoulder and a huge bowie knife in a scabbard on the other shoulder. At his waist he carried a brace of Colt .45s.

"So, you are the *gringo* who has come to ride for Don Soltano?" Luis Ortiz asked. He smiled broadly. "It will be a pleasure to take your money, señor."

"I have not come to ride for him," Slocum said as he settled into the empty chair. "Does that mean you don't want any of my money?"

Ortiz and the others at the table laughed heartily. "I'll take your money, *señor,* no matter who you are riding for."

Slocum bought twenty-five dollars' worth of chips. That sum represented half of his total resources. If he lost it he would still have enough to get back to the States, even if he never collected his money. If he won, it would make the wait for his money a little less agonizing.

Slocum drew the deal and shuffled the cards. The deck was old and well-used, but as he shuffled he felt for telltale signs of marking and could find none. His hands moved swiftly, folding the cards in and out, until

the law of random numbers became king of the table.
He shoved the deck toward Ortiz, who cut the cards,
then pushed them back.

"And now, *gringo,* we shall see if luck is on your
side," Ortiz said.

Slocum quickly became lost in the game. Ortiz might
be a dangerous enemy in a range war, but at this table
he was merely a mathematical problem to be solved. A
problem that became more acute when, several hands
into the game, Ortiz made a rather substantial raise.

John looked at his hand. He held three tens and two
fives. He had discarded the ace of spades to draw the
third ten, and he was reasonably certain that the risk of
calling was worth taking. He had to be sure, though,
because he had no more money on the table. If he called
his bet he would have to go into his last twenty-five
dollars. Perhaps, he considered, the sensible thing to do
would be to fold. But he couldn't fold. He was certain
this was a winning hand. Finally he pulled out the twenty-
five dollars he had put back and laid it on the pile of
money which was stacked in the center of the table.

"I call," he said. He studied Ortiz's eyes as he put the
money down, then, when he saw them narrow slightly,
he knew he had won. Ortiz, not seeing any more money
in front of Slocum, had tried to buy the pot.

"*Carajole!*" Ortiz shouted, and he threw his cards on
the table and got up, then stamped over to the bar. He
turned and looked back at Slocum as Slocum raked in
the money. There was over one hundred fifty dollars in
the pot, roughly three times what Slocum had when he
arrived. With this much money he could afford to wait
for Soltano.

"*Señor* Ortiz, I thank you for your contribution,"
Slocum said, stacking the chips in little piles before him.

"We will meet again, Slocum," Ortiz said angrily.

"If it is as profitable as this meeting, Ortiz, I'll look forward to it," Slocum answered back.

"I think it will not be so profitable for you," Ortiz muttered. Then, still cursing, Ortiz poured himself a stiff drink as Slocum took his chips to the bartender to cash them in.

"Thanks, gents," Slocum called out as he pushed his way through the beaded door.

"The *gringo* is very lucky," one of the other players said.

"I think his luck will run out soon," Ortiz promised.

Slocum started back to the hotel. Tonight Linda had promised she would come to see him, and he had to admit that he was looking forward to it, particularly after the little episode earlier in the afternoon.

The sun had set while Slocum played cards. Now it was very dark in the little village. Slocum had learned his lesson the night before, and now he walked well away from the buildings so that, if anyone was so inclined, they wouldn't have an easy shot at him. He studied the shadows closely, thinking that this might well be the darkest town at night he had ever been in. Once, he stopped, and his hand dropped to his Colt. He cocked his pistol, the metallic click making a deadly sound in the night.

Slocum wasn't sure he had seen anything. It was really too dark to be certain. But his sense of danger warned him, and he stood poised for a long, silent moment, every nerve ending strained and ready. Then, though he didn't see the danger recede any more than he had seen it appear, he sensed that whoever was waiting for him had withdrawn. He eased the hammer down on his pistol and walked on to his hotel.

The clerk was sitting at a small table behind the desk, eating a supper of beans and tortillas. He looked up as Slocum entered, saw who it was, and returned to his meal.

"Any messages for me, *amigo*?" Slocum asked. "Maybe a package from Don Soltano?"

"*Nada, señor,*" the clerk answered.

"*Gracias.*" Slocum climbed the narrow stairway to his room, then, standing to one side of his door, pushed it open. He didn't really think anyone was waiting in his room to ambush him, but he wasn't taking any more chances in this place.

His room was empty, so he stepped in, walked over to the window, and looked out before he lit the candle. He could see the street below and the roof of the building next door. He watched for a long, silent moment to see if there was any unexpected movement, but saw nothing. Maybe he was being too jumpy. Slocum lit the candle and lay back on his bed to wait for Linda.

He had been back in his room less than half an hour when there was a quiet knock on the door. He smiled and moved quickly to open it, to let Linda in. The smile froze on his face, because there stood not only Linda, but her brother as well.

"Please, John, let us in quickly before anyone sees us," Linda pleaded.

The sense of urgency Linda projected overcame any disappointment Slocum had over the fact she hadn't come alone. He stepped back from the door and Linda and her brother moved quickly into the room, then closed the door behind them.

"What is it?" Slocum asked. "What's wrong?" By second nature, Slocum moved them away from the door and the window. If there really was any danger now, those were the two places where they could be threatened.

"They have come," Joaquin said.

"They have come? Who has come?"

"The *gringos*," Joaquin said. "The gunfighters."

"The Americans my father hired to fight his battle," Linda said. "They arrived today. They were at the ranch when I returned."

"So they're here already," Slocum said. He was disappointed. He had hoped to have his business all settled with Soltano before the Americans arrived. "Are you sure it's them?"

"I'm sure," Linda said. "They are all Americans, and there are six of them, just as my father said there would be."

"Yes, six of them," Joaquin said. "Each one more evil than the other."

"Names, man. Do you know any names?"

"No," Joaquin admitted.

"I know one name," Linda said. "He is the one who leads them. His name is Dave something. Dave Ross? No, that's not it."

"Rawls? Dave Rawls?" Slocum asked.

"*Sí*. Dave Rawls. Do you know him?"

"I don't know him, but I know of him," Slocum replied. He thought back to a night in Dodge City the year before. He had heard gunplay in a saloon, rushed in to find Toby Mitchell stretched out on the floor, spilling blood from a couple of bullet holes in his chest. Toby Mitchell was good with a gun, one of the best Slocum had ever known. It was quite a shock to see him lying there.

"The feller's fast, John," Toby had said, coughing up flecks of blood as he tried to talk. "Don't believe I ever saw one as fast."

The man Toby was talking about was Dave Rawls. Rawls was gone by the time Slocum arrived on the scene, but he had left his mark. Slocum saw to Toby's burying, sent his gun, holster, and saddle to a brother who lived down in Texas.

Slocum had heard Rawls's name mentioned on a few other occasions too. Dave Rawls was building quite a name for himself all along the owlhoot trail. Now it seemed to be paying off for Rawls, as his reputation had earned him a position in Soltano's private army.

"Yeah, I've heard of him," Slocum said. "He's a gun-runner, rustler, and murderer. He fits the pattern of the type of man your father would hire."

Suddenly there was an explosion of glass as something came flying through the window of Slocum's room. Thinking it might be a bomb, he grabbed Linda and her brother and shoved them roughly to the floor behind the bed, then dived down with them.

"Look out!" he called.

They lay that way for a couple of seconds, then Slocum saw what had come sailing through the window. It wasn't a bomb; it was nothing but a rock, to which a matchbox had been tied.

"What is it?" Linda asked in a frightened voice.

"I don't know," Slocum admitted. He stared at the rock and the matchbox for a few more seconds, until he was convinced that was all it was. Then he reached out and slid the rock close. He untied the matchbox and shook it. Something rattled inside.

"It just looks like a box," Joaquin said.

"It is a box," Slocum agreed. "But there's something

in it." He took the box over to the table, where a candle stood under a wavering flame, illuminating the room. There, he opened it. A single .45-caliber bullet fell out of the box and bounced on the table.

"It's a bullet," Linda said with a look of curiosity.

"Why would anyone send me a bullet?" Slocum muttered, mostly to himself, picking up the shiny piece and examining it cautiously.

"Look," Linda said. "There's something scratched on the bullet."

Slocum examined the soft lead and saw that Linda was right.

Slocum, para ti, gringo puerco.

"What does it mean?" he asked them, as he read over the Spanish inscription.

Joaquin took the bullet. "This is a bullet with your name on it," he said. "It says . . . 'for you, *gringo* pig.'"

"Any idea who might have sent this?"

"It could be anyone," Joaquin said. "It could be someone from Delgado, because they think you are allied with my father . . . or it could even be my father, because you won't allow yourself to be bought by him."

"Whoever it is, they seem to be going an extra mile to let me know I'm not welcome here," Slocum concluded.

"Do you think maybe it is some sort of joke?" Linda asked.

"It is no joke," Joaquin warned.

"I agree with your brother," Slocum said, shaking his head. "If it is a joke, it is one without humor. I'm taking it seriously." He put the bullet in his pocket. "And I thank you for telling me that Rawls and his bunch have arrived."

"John, remember, you said you would take us with you," Linda reminded him. "I have brought my brother with me. I want to take my mother, too."

"Your mother?"

"*Sí.*"

"I thought you said your mother wouldn't leave."

"I think she will go now, *Señor* Slocum," Joaquin answered for his sister. "She was beaten again today," he added bitterly.

"I think maybe something was broken, this time," Linda said. "I have sent for a doctor, but I do not know when he can see her."

"Maybe you can look at her?" Joaquin suggested.

"Me? I'm not a doctor."

"I know you are not a doctor. But you are a man who has seen much violence. A man who has seen much violence has learned to know when someone is badly hurt. Is this not true?"

"I reckon I can tell if a person is all busted up inside about as well as most doctors," Slocum agreed. "But that doesn't mean I can do anything about it."

"When someone is that badly hurt, can even a doctor do anything?" Joaquin asked.

"No," Slocum agreed. "I reckon not."

"Then you will be as valuable as a doctor," Joaquin pointed out. "Will you look at her?"

"All right. I'll do what I can."

"And if she can ride, you will bring her back with you so she can be with us?" Linda asked.

"Bring her with me? Aren't you going back to the ranch?"

"Never!" Linda spat angrily.

"On this, my sister and I completely agree," Joaquin said. "We have seen our father for the last time. We wish to leave this accursed place. If you will take us."

"I'll take you," Slocum promised. He sighed. "But I want to warn you, I'm not going anywhere until I get my money. Dave Rawls or no Dave Rawls. I'm going to confront Don Eduardo and get what's due me."

"Be careful," Linda said softly.

Slocum examined the soft lead and saw that Linda was right.

Linda put her hand on Slocum's arm, and he felt the heat of her fingers. For a moment he recalled their time together earlier, recalled what they had felt then, and he knew that she was recalling it as well, because her eyes showed light, way down deep.

"You are a good man, John Slocum," Linda said. "Perhaps things will yet work out for us."

"I'll get you out of here," Slocum promised. "I'm going to get my money——"

"And my mother," Linda reminded her.

"And your mother," Slocum added. "We can leave in the morning."

Linda smiled. "That will be nice," she said. She looked over to Slocum's bed and saw the dirty clothes he had taken off before bathing. She pointed to them.

"If we are leaving in the morning, you should leave with clean clothes. Give those to me. I will wash them for you."

"You are a *doña*," Slocum said. "I can't let you do my laundry."

"Please, I want to do this. I am not too proud to wash your clothes. Let me do them. I'll bring them back in the morning."

"All right," Slocum said, gathering the dirty clothes and handing them to Linda. "You've cooked a meal for me, and you're doing my laundry. What's left?"

Linda looked around toward her brother, and saw that he had already stepped out into the hall to wait for her. She turned back to Slocum and planted a quick kiss on his lips.

"When I have the opportunity, I will show you what is left," she promised.

8

The moon hung high in the night sky, painting the landscape in hues of silver and black. It was an exceptionally bright moon, and the visibility was almost as good as daytime.

A jackrabbit popped up from the brush beside the road, ran in great, bounding leaps alongside Slocum, then turned and skittered out across the rocky ground toward another growth of brush.

An owl hooted.

Slocum thought of Linda as he rode toward his meeting with her father. He should have known when he first saw her that she meant trouble, but she boiled his blood whenever she looked at him with those hot Spanish eyes. And now he was mixed up in her life, whether he wanted to be or not. He was committed to taking her and her brother, and now her mother, away from this place, when all he really wanted to do was get his money and get the hell out of here.

Half an hour later Slocum swung down from his horse in front of the Hacienda del Soltano. He led his horse over to a watering trough and let the animal drink before he tied it to the hitching rail.

There was something wrong. He should have been greeted, if not in a friendly welcome, then at least in a challenge. Soltano was engaged in a range war, had even brought in guns from the States, and yet no one was standing watch. It hardly seemed the way to fight a war.

Slocum started toward the big house, heard a burst of laughter from the bunkhouse, and looked that way.

"You rotten son of a bitch!" someone shouted. The words were spoken by an American. Men had been killed for saying less, but this sobriquet was obviously launched in the raucous fun which had brought on the first laughter, because it was followed immediately by more laughter. The six Americans Soltano had hired were all there, but they were doing nothing to earn their pay. They were in the bunkhouse, obviously drinking and lolling around. Expensive hands, Slocum thought, to be lying around doing nothing.

Slocum walked across the front courtyard, still un-challenged except by a little spotted dog who ran up to sniff around his legs, before it ran back behind the barn without giving so much as one bark. Even the chickens, which had squawked at him on his first visit, the day he arrived, were quiet and down for the night.

Slocum passed under the colonnade and breathed the scent of wisteria and honeysuckle as he approached the main house. There was nothing visible which would give him the idea that this was anything more than a very beautiful and peaceful hacienda and yet, even as he stood there, he had a feeling in the back of his neck, in the palms of his hands, that something was wrong. There was something not quite right about the Hacienda del Soltano.

Slocum pulled on a rope, and a bell rang from somewhere in the house. A moment later Filomena opened the door. She gasped when she saw him.

"*Señor!* What are you doing here?"

"I've come to see Soltano," Slocum said firmly. "And his wife."

"His wife?"

"Yes."

"I don't understand, *señor.* Why do you wish to see his wife?"

"Linda and Joaquin said she was beaten today. They asked me to check on her."

Filomena looked down toward the floor quickly, as if frightened to meet his gaze.

"Who is it?" Don Eduardo called from another room. "Who is here?"

"It is *Señor* Juan Slocum," the old *duenna* called back.

"Slocum?" A moment later, Soltano stood at the door of that room and looked toward Slocum. A candle sconce clung to the wall just beside him, its wavering flame casting a flickering red glow over Soltano's face, creating vivid contrasts in light and shadow. Soltano's eyes were deeply shaded, his cheeks shining, his lips gleaming red in the candlelight. For an instant he could have been an apparition from hell . . . the devil incarnate. Soltano moved on into the room and the light which fell on him changed, breaking the spell. He became a man again, though it was obvious to see that he was a man who was greatly agitated.

"Where is my daughter?" Soltano hissed through tightly

pressed lips. "Where is my son?"

"Why ask me?"

"Because you know," Soltano insisted. "I heard you mention their names to Filomena. I demand that you tell me where they are."

"Your son and daughter are both grown," Slocum answered without raising his voice. "I guess they're where they want to be."

"They should be here!" Soltano shouted, emphasizing his point by driving a fist into his open hand. "Here! I need them."

"You need them? Why do you need them?"

"Because their mother, my . . . dear . . . wife," he went on, putting his hand to his forehead, "is dead."

The revelation shocked Slocum, and he looked at Soltano in surprise. "My God! Linda said she had been badly beaten, said she thought something was broken inside her, but she didn't know how bad. You son of a bitch! You beat your own wife to death?"

"What? No, no, I didn't do that," Soltano said, in a shocked voice. "You must know I could never do such a thing."

"That's not what Linda and Joaquin think."

"Linda and Joaquin are mistaken. They do not understand. I loved my wife, I loved her dearly. I would never do anything to hurt her."

"Like hell you wouldn't. She's dead, isn't she?"

"She was ill. She was a very sick woman, only she didn't want our children to know. Where are they? They should be here with their mother."

"Too late for that, but I'll tell them. What happens then is up to them."

"I insist that you tell me where they are," Soltano demanded. "Tell me now."

"It's none of your business where they are," Slocum replied. "And the only business you have with me is the money you owe me. I'd like to be paid, Don Soltano. Now."

"Tomorrow," Don Eduardo countered. "Tomorrow. Can't you see I am in mourning?"

Slocum took a deep breath. He was about to press the issue, but decided against it. He would give Soltano more time.

"All right, one more day," Slocum agreed. "I'll be out here tomorrow. You just be sure you have it."

"I'll have it, I'll have it,' Soltano promised.

Slocum started to leave, then he turned back to Soltano. "About your men," he said. "The Americans you hired to fight for you."

"What about them?"

"It's none of my business," Slocum told Soltano, "but if I had paid good money for a private army, I'd want at least one of them standing watch. They're all out in the bunkhouse, drunk, unless I miss my guess. Nobody even stuck his head out the door to see who I was."

"They work for me," Soltano growled back. "I'll take care of things. I don't need any advice from a *gringo* who won't even join me in the fight."

"Whatever you say, Don Soltano," Slocum said easily. "Just have the money for me in the morning."

Slocum walked back toward the entry foyer of the house. As soon as he got there, the old *duenna* stepped out from the shadows of the hall where she had been waiting. Her sudden appearance startled him.

"You ought to be more careful about doing things like that," Slocum cautioned.

"I must speak with you."

"What about?"

"To tell you to be careful, *señor*," she warned. "The shadow of death follows you this night. Guard well the daughter of this family."

Before Slocum could ask her what she was talking about, she withdrew back into the shadows once more, then walked quickly down the long hall to get away from him.

Slocum went outside, then through the blossom-perfumed air to his horse. As he untied it from the hitching rail, he heard another burst of laughter from the bunkhouse. With the mistress of the house lying dead inside, these men were not only incompetent, they were insensitive.

"You do not join your *amigos, señor?*" The man who spoke was standing in the shadow of a tree. He appeared to be in his late fifties or early sixties, with a large belly and a round face.

"They aren't my *amigos*," Slocum replied.

"You are the one they call Slocum?"

"Yes."

"I am called Bustamante. You may ask the *señorita* about me. I am her friend."

"What can I do for you, Bustamante?"

Bustamante looked over his shoulder toward the big house, then out toward the bunkhouse. Another burst of laughter rolled out from the bunkhouse.

"Tell the *señorita* not to come back to this place," Bustamante said. "There is death in this place."

"You mean her mother?"

"The *señora* is only the beginning. Many will die before this business is done."

"I doubt there will even be a range war," Slocum said. "When Delgado sees all the guns Soltano has hired, he'll lose his appetite for fighting."

"I am not talking about war with *Señor* Delgado."

Slocum was confused by Bustamante's remark. "What are you talking about?"

"Death, *señor*. Much death. Please, do not let the *señorita* return to this place."

The door to the bunkhouse opened, and one of the Americans stepped outside. Bustamante looked over in fear, then drew farther back into the shadows.

"I must go," he said softly. "Remember my warning."

"I'll remember."

The ride back to Santa Luz was without incident. Slocum stopped several times and listened for signs that he was being followed, but he heard no one. Once he left the trail and climbed up a towering rock outcropping. From this elevated vantage point, and under the bright, silver moon, he could see all the way back to the Soltano Rancho. He watched for several minutes until he was absolutely satisfied that no one followed him.

Slocum thought of Linda and Joaquin, back in the village. He would have to tell them about their mother's death. It wasn't a task he looked forward to, but it was one that needed to be done.

Linda and Joaquin were both waiting at the head of the stairs when Slocum returned to the hotel.

"Did you see her?" Linda asked impatiently. "Did you see my mother?"

"How is she? Will she be able to come with us?" added Joaquin.

Slocum shook his head sadly.

There was something in Slocum's eyes, something in the way he shook his head, which conveyed the message to Linda. She perceived it before Joaquin, and she gasped in fear.

"John, what is it?" Linda asked. "What's wrong?"

"It's your mother," Slocum said softly. "I'm sorry, Linda, Joaquin. She's dead."

"Dead?" Linda asked in a small, weak voice.

"Yes."

Tears leaped to Linda's eyes, and Slocum put his arms around her to comfort her. "I'm sorry," he said. "I'm sorry to be the one to tell you this."

"He killed her," Joaquin blurted out, his own eyes shining as he fought against the tears which were welling there. "My father killed her."

"He says he didn't," Slocum said. "He says your mother was ill, but she didn't want you to know."

"The only illness my mother suffered was the illness of being beaten by my father," Joaquin replied.

Linda turned away from them for a moment, then turned back. "I'm going out there. I'm going to see her. I'm going out there now, tonight."

"I don't know," Slocum said in a concerned tone. "Your father wants you out there, but I don't know if that's a good idea or not. What do you know about a man named Bustamante? Can he be trusted?"

"Bustamante? He is my friend," Linda answered at once. "He takes care of my horses."

"Bustamante can be trusted, *Señor* Slocum." Joaquin agreed. "He has been on the ranch since the days of my grandfather. Why do you ask?"

"Bustamante said not to let Linda come out to the ranch. He was very serious about it."

"Bustamante is right, Linda," Joaquin said. "I don't think you should go."

"We can't just leave our mother out there without even going to see her," Linda insisted. "I won't leave her there, alone, all night."

"You won't have to. I'll go," Joaquin promised. "I'll see her tonight, and make arrangements to have her brought into town tomorrow."

"We'll both go."

"No," Joaquin insisted. "Linda, you must stay here. I fear that it isn't safe for you. I'll see her for both of us."

"If you trust Bustamante and your brother, you should listen to them," Slocum advised her. "The Americans are out there now. I don't know any of them, but I don't like the feel of it."

"Pooh! What can they do?" Linda asked.

"My sister, if you do not know the evil things bad men can do to a girl, that is all the more reason you shouldn't go," Joaquin urged.

Linda sighed. "All right," she finally agreed. "All right, I won't go. But you must promise me that you will have her brought into town tomorrow."

"This I promise you," Joaquin said. He looked at Slocum. "*Señor* Slocum, would it be possible for me to borrow your horse tonight? I'm afraid that the horse I rode to town is lame."

"Yes, of course you can use my horse."

"You'll look out for my sister?"

"I'll look out for her," Slocum promised.

Shortly after Joaquin left for the ranch, Linda returned to her own room and Slocum went to bed. He slept, but he slept fitfully, and when the quiet knock came at his door a few hours later, he heard it at once. He got out of bed, moved quickly to the door, and opened it. Linda was standing in the hall with a dressing gown wrapped around her.

"I'm sorry if I have disturbed you, John Slocum," she

said in a small, weak voice. "But I don't want to be alone tonight. Please let me come in."

"Of course," Slocum said, stepping back to let her pass. "I'll light a candle."

"No," Linda said, putting her hand on his arm. "No, you don't need to do that."

"Are you all right?" Slocum asked.

"Yes." She put her hand to her forehead. "No," she amended. "I'm not all right. Oh, John, I feel so alone now . . . so abandoned. I need someone . . . someone to hold me, someone to make me feel needed." She put her arms around Slocum and pressed her body against his. Slocum could feel the heat of her body, the urgent thrust of her breasts against his chest. He recalled the sight of those breasts during the picnic and he recalled the unfulfilled arousal they had caused. The warm coals of desire began heating up again, but this was not the time for such feelings, so he tried to force the fires back down.

"Linda," Slocum said softly. "Linda, this isn't right. I feel like I'm taking advantage of you."

"No," she said. "I'm taking advantage of you. Of your goodness, and your kindness."

"Yeah," Slocum choked. "But right now I don't feel good and kind. Right now I feel—"

"I know how you feel," Linda interrupted. "I feel the same way." She leaned into him then and kissed him with hot, hungry lips.

Slocum had a passing thought to resist her, but almost before it was born, he felt himself giving in to her. Her kiss burned through to his very core, and he felt her tongue probing first gently, then eagerly into his mouth. Finally, the kiss ended, and Slocum pulled his lips away. He continued to hold her, though, and her body trembled in his embrace.

"I've been driven mad with desire for you, John Slocum," Linda whispered, breathing hard. "From the moment we met...from the moment I first saw you in my father's house, I knew that I wanted you. Please, I need you now, more than ever. Make love to me, John Slocum."

Slocum picked Linda up and carried her over to his bed. She was helpless...helpless before his virile strength and helpless before her own flaming passions. She opened her dressing gown, and he could see by the splash of moonlight through the window that she had come to him nearly naked. It required only the one quick move and she was ready for him.

Slocum came to her naked, his manhood thrust out in front of him like a sword. Linda gasped when she saw it, and she reached out to touch it.

"It's...it's so big," she whispered. "And hot, and throbbing. It's as if it has a life of its own."

"At times like this, it nearly does," Slocum admitted.

"John?" Her voice was small, almost childlike.

"Yes?" He was kissing her now, moving his lips from her neck down to her shoulders, then on to her breasts, feeling the smooth, warm skin of her breasts, and the firm texture of her nipples.

"John, I've...I've never done this before. You don't mind?"

Slocum raised his lips from her nipple. "Are you sure you want to?"

"Yes!" Linda said. "Oh, yes, you must. If you stop now, I'll die of want. Please, you must go on."

"All right," Slocum said. "But you'll have to help. If you've never done this before, we'll have to be very gentle."

"You'll be gentle," Linda said. "I've never known

anyone more gentle or tender than you."

Gently, tenderly, Slocum moved himself into position. He kissed her, and when he did, he felt himself slip inside.

"Ohhh," she moaned. "Oh, yes, I knew it would be like this. Don't stop. Go on. Please go on!"

Slocum pushed, moving with a gentle, yet firm pressure. Linda, growing impatient with the barrier that was preventing her from taking him all the way, thrust her hips resolutely, then gasped at the sharp, but quickly receding pain.

Slocum was all the way inside now, sliding in and out in long thrusts. Several times he approached the precipice, but each time he backed away, prolonging the delicious agony of the quest. He felt her building, then launching herself into orgasm with the joyful abandon of a woman who is experiencing rapture for the first time. She exploded beneath him, writhing and thrusting, moaning and nibbling at his neck, thrashing her hands on his back, grinding her pelvis against him, as she melted into the heat of her climax.

From somewhere in his spine, his toes, and the back of his head, Slocum felt himself dissolving, turning to boiling essence. This time he made no effort to hold back. He plunged deep inside her as he boiled over, and Linda, realizing what was happening, bucked against him one final time.

9

Slocum rolled the tortilla in his fingers and, using it like a spoon, scooped up the last of his breakfast beans. He washed the food down with a drink of strong, black coffee, then topped the breakfast off with a smoke, lighting the quirly just as Linda came through the front door of the cafe. He smiled at her.

"Good morning," he said. The smile left his lips as she got closer to his table, because he saw that her face was pinched, her eyes worried. This wasn't sadness over her mother, this was a new worry. "What is it?" he asked.

"John, I'm worried about Joaquin. Have you seen him this morning?"

"No," Slocum admitted.

"He should be back by now. He should have been back long ago."

"I'm sure there's nothing wrong," Slocum said. "It's probably taking some time to make all the arrangements.

He'll be in before noon, I'm certain."

"I'm not so sure," Linda said in a worried voice. "I have this feeling. . . ." She laughed nervously. "I know you won't understand, but ever since we were children, Joaquin and I have been able to tell what the other is thinking or feeling. We even used to get ill together. Now I have a terrible feeling that Joaquin is in danger . . . or worse. I know you must think this is silly," she added.

"No, I don't," Slocum admitted to her. "I know about those feelings. They've kept me alive more than once. Look, would you like me to take you out to the ranch? We could check on him."

"Oh, would you?" Linda said. "Yes, I'd really appreciate that. I'm very worried about him."

Slocum drained the rest of his coffee, then left money on the table for his food. "Oh, I almost forgot. Do you want to eat breakfast?" he asked.

"No. No, I'm fine." Linda said. "I just want to find my brother, that's all."

"I need to go out there anyway," Slocum said. "Your father promised he would pay me this morning."

"I hope he keeps his promise."

"He'll keep it," Slocum said. "I'll see to that. I'll have to rent a horse at the livery. Joaquin still has mine."

"No need. We can go in my sulky," Linda suggested. "It's being hitched up now, if you're ready."

"Let's go," Slocum said, picking up his hat and starting for the door.

They walked down to the livery stable where Linda's sulky stood out front, the team already hitched up, the horses switching their tails at the flies which buzzed around their rumps. The old liveryman handed Slocum the reins after he climbed into the seat.

"*Señor,* you have not seen my brother this morning, have you?" Linda asked.

"No, I have not seen him," the liveryman answered, looking down at the ground.

"If he comes in, tell him to wait in town for us," Slocum said.

"*Sí,* I will tell him."

Slocum snapped the reins against the matched team, and the horses, glad to be moving away from the flies buzzing around the stable, stepped out briskly. They pulled the sulky out of town, moving in a graceful but ground-eating gait which had them two miles from town within ten minutes.

"John Slocum," Linda said, pressing her leg against his. He could feel the heat of her body even through the clothes they wore. "I want to thank you for last night."

Slocum chuckled. "That ought to be going the other way around, Linda," he said. "I'm the one should be doing the thanking."

Linda put her hand on Slocum's arm and squeezed it. "I've never known anything so wonderful," she said. "Is it always so wonderful?"

"It can be if it's right," Slocum said. "Sometimes it's not right. Then it can wind up getting people in a lot of trouble. You want to be careful about things like that."

Linda giggled. "I feel like you are my teacher."

"I guess in a way I am," Slocum agreed. "It's always good to—" Slocum suddenly interrupted his sentence and hauled back on the reins. When the sulky stopped, he stood up and looked down the road. There was something lying in the road, something black and still.

"John," Linda said in a frightened voice. "John, what is it?"

"I don't know," Slocum answered. "But I don't like the way it looks." He snapped the reins and the team broke into a quick trot. As they drew closer he realized what it was and so did Linda, because she cried out.

"Oh! John! It's Joaquin!"

Slocum stopped the rig, jumped down, and ran toward the figure on the ground. "Maybe you better stay back," he cautioned.

Despite his attempt to get Linda to stay in the buggy, she went with him. Joaquin was lying in the dirt of the road, a little pool of blood beside him. Slocum's horse was nearby, grazing, still saddled, reins trailing.

"John! He's been shot!" Linda cried again.

Slocum knelt down beside Joaquin and put his hand on the boy's neck. He could feel the pulse, felt the boy work his neck as he breathed.

"He's still alive," Slocum told Linda. "I'll load him into the sulky and we'll take him to the ranch."

"Joaquin! Joaquin, it's me, Linda!"

Joaquin opened his eyes and smiled weakly at Linda.

"I knew you would come," he said. "I lay here for a long time, waiting, but I knew you would come."

"Who shot you?" Slocum asked. "One of Delgado's men?"

Joaquin shook his head no, and tried to speak, but bright red blood flecked the corners of his mouth. Slocum had seen enough wounds like that to know what it meant. The bullet had penetrated the lungs. Joaquin would die no matter how quickly they got him to a doctor.

"Oh, Joaquin!" Linda said as she dabbed at his mouth with her scarf.

"It wasn't one of Delgado's men? Who, then?" Slocum asked.

"The *gringo*, Rawls," Joaquin gasped.

The effort of speaking seemed too much for Joaquin and he began a spasm of coughing. Finally, with a gasping rattle, he stiffened, then grew still.

"Joaquin? Joaquin?" Linda shouted, and when she got no response, she let out an agonized cry. "Joaquin!"

Slocum put his hand on the young man's neck, felt for a pulse.

"I'm sorry," he said sadly. "He's dead."

"No! No!" Linda called, and her body was wracked with sobs.

Slocum put his arms around her and let her cry on his shoulder for several moments until she was able to regain control of herself.

"Let's go," he said. "We'll take him home."

Slocum tied his horse to the back of the sulky, then drove the team the rest of the way to the Soltano ranch.

"Oh, why did my father ever bring these evil men down here?" Linda asked. "If he had not brought them here, my brother would still be alive. I want to see the look on his face when I tell him."

Slocum looked over at Linda, at her tear-stained face, but he said nothing to her. He, too, was thinking about the irony of Joaquin being killed by one of his father's men. Then he remembered last night, the behavior of the Americans, and the warning of Bustamante. He began putting a few things together in his mind, and he didn't like the picture that emerged. Maybe he was too suspicious. Maybe the fact that Joaquin was killed by one of his father's men was just a tragic coincidence. Or maybe it wasn't a coincidence at all.

Slocum noticed the difference as soon as he turned through the gate. The corral was empty, for one thing . . . for another, there was no one in sight. The Americans who had been so boisterous in the bunkhouse the night before were conspicuously absent. Even the Mexicans seemed to be gone. One lone chicken squawked and fluttered across the courtyard in front of them as Slocum halted the team.

"Where is Manuel?" Linda asked.

"Who?"

"Manuel Bustamante," Linda said. "You met him last night, remember? He is in charge of these horses. He treats them as if they are his own, and every time I return he is here to meet me, to see to the animals. Why isn't he out here to meet me now?"

"I don't know," Slocum replied, still looking around. "In fact, there are several things that don't seem right. Come on, I'll take Joaquin inside the house."

Slocum scooped Linda's dead brother up into his arms, then walked up the long colonnade to the front door. Linda opened the door for him and they went inside. Slocum carried the young man's body over to a sofa and stretched him out. After he put the boy down, he rose up and looked around. The house seemed unusually quiet and empty.

"Where is everyone?" he asked.

"I don't know. My father should be here. Filomena should have greeted us at the door. Filomena? Filomena," she called. "It's me, Linda."

There was a scraping from another room, then a crashing sound. Linda started toward the noise with Slocum right behind her. As soon as they reached the door they saw Filomena lying on the floor of the other room. The crash had come from an overturned table and a big vase, smashed when Filomena fell. Filomena's face was bruised and battered.

"Filomena! Filomena, what's wrong? What happened

to you?" Linda shouted, then quickly knelt beside the old woman.

Filomena began speaking, jabbering in anguished Spanish. Slocum tried to listen, but she was so upset and speaking so rapidly that he couldn't understand a word she said. Finally, when she had gasped out her entire story, Linda translated it for Slocum, bathing the old woman's face with a dampened cloth as she did so.

"It was the Americans," she said. "Dave Rawls and the others. Like you, they asked my father for money. Unlike you, they were not willing to wait. They forced him to open the safe and they took his money." Linda laughed bitterly. "It seems they had no intention of fighting for my father. They just used that as an excuse to come down here and rob him. It serves my father right. Perhaps now he has learned a lesson."

This was the thought that had troubled Slocum earlier. He had not wanted to voice it because he didn't want to worry Linda in case it wasn't true. Now, tragically, it was all too true.

Filomena spoke again, in a soft, apologetic voice.

"Are you sure?" Linda asked in a soft voice, asking the question in English.

"Sí," the old woman answered.

"What is it?" Slocum asked. "What did she say?"

Linda took a deep breath and continued to wipe the old woman's face for a few more moments. She was silent for a long time.

"Linda?" Slocum asked again.

"It's my father," Linda finally said. "Filomena said that the men, the Americans, shot him when they robbed him. Filomena says my father is dead."

Slocum put his hand on Linda's shoulder and she leaned against it.

"Some people draw bad cards in bunches, Linda," he said kindly. "You seem to have drawn all of them. Your mother last night, then your brother, and now your father. Where is your father? Did she say?"

Linda asked Filomena, and Filomena answered in soft, injured tones.

"He is in the front room," Linda told Slocum.

Slocum squeezed her gently, then walked through the big house. He couldn't help but notice the tapestry on the walls, the beautiful furniture, the carpets, the exquisite tiles, the vases and other works of art. The Hacienda del Soltano was a castle. And yet Don Soltano was a man of such greed and powerful, driving ambition that he was not content to enjoy the beauty that was already around him. Instead he drove, stole, lied, and cheated to get more. Why? Slocum wondered about it. What would he have bought if he had gained more money? Another vase, perhaps? A new carpet? What a mockery all the finery seemed now. What a quiet, hollow mockery.

Slocum stopped at the door to a big room and looked inside. Furniture was turned over and smashed, the upholstery and even the wallpaper was slashed. The room was an absolute shambles. Against the far wall stood a large steel safe. The door of the safe was standing wide open. Papers and other items had been pulled out and strewn about on the floor. If there had been any money in the safe, it was all gone now.

At first Slocum didn't see Soltano, but when he took a step inside, he saw Linda's father sprawled out on the floor in front of the safe. He moved quickly to the don, but he could tell even before he reached him that he was dead. There was a certain slackness to the don's feet, a grotesque twist to one of the man's hands, which indicated that Eduardo Soltano, a prince in life, was now so much dead meat.

Slocum knelt beside the body and looked at it. Soltano had been shot in the back of the head, just as if he had been executed. In fact, he could see now that Soltano had been shot while he was on his knees. Had they made him beg for his life? Had they subjected him to a final humiliation before they killed him? Nobody deserved to die this way, not even a man like Soltano.

"Soltano, I confess I didn't care much for you," Slocum said quietly. "But your son seemed to have some good stuff in him, and your daughter is a good woman, so I reckon that somewhere, deep down inside, you had to have something good about you. It was just hard to find, that's all."

Slocum saw something lying on the floor next to Soltano's body and he picked it up. It was another .45 caliber bullet, just like the one that had been thrown through Slocum's window the previous night. This bullet too, had something scratched into the lead. Only this time, Slocum didn't need an interpreter to read it for him. This time there was only one word:

SLOCUM.

Slocum put this bullet in his pocket with the other one.

10

Slocum returned to the room where Linda cared for Filomena. The old woman was sitting at a table with a glass of tequila in front of her. As she sipped the drink she made no excuses and she drank the liquor with the authority of one who, despite her earlier protestations to the contrary, was well experienced in handling it.

"Did you find him?" Linda asked. Her voice was calm now. She had encountered too much grief in the last twelve hours and was unable to assimilate any more. Now the protective mechanisms of her mind had taken over. Slocum was glad about that. An excessively grieving or, worse yet, hysterical woman would make his job much more difficult now.

"Yes," Slocum answered clearly. "I found him." Without asking, Slocum poured himself a glass of tequila, drank it down, felt its controlled fire on his tongue.

"I must make all the arrangements," Linda said calmly.

"I have an entire family to bury."

"You've had quite a burden put on your shoulders, Linda. But, from what I've seen of you, you're strong enough to carry it." Slocum put his hand gently on Linda's shoulder, then looked at the old woman.

"Never has there been a stronger or better woman than my Linda," Filomena said proudly. She poured a second glass of tequila.

Slocum watched without accusation as the old woman drank tequila from a water tumbler. She had been through a lot, he reasoned, and if tequila could help her through it, more power to her.

"*Señora* Calderon, do you have any idea where the *gringos* went? Perhaps you may have overheard one of them say something," Slocum said quietly.

Filomena shook her head slowly. "I do not know," she answered. "I think they may have taken the horses. I heard one of them laugh and say something about how good it was of the don to provide them with such fine horses."

"They did take the horses," Slocum said in a tone of controlled anger. "There are none left on the place."

"Filomena, do you know where Manuel is?" Linda asked. "He did not come to greet me as I arrived."

"No," Filomena said, shaking her head. "I have seen no one on this place since the *gringos* left."

"Perhaps the others left with the Americans," Slocum suggested. "Or ran away."

"Some may have joined the Americans," Linda conceded. "Since the trouble, the war with Delgado, my father has not always hired the most responsible of men. But you met Manuel Bustamante last night. Do you think he would run away, or join the Americans?"

"No," Slocum admitted. "I don't believe he would."

"Please, John, try to find him for me." Linda put her hand to her forehead and looked around. "I . . . I will need help. I have many things to do and Manuel can help me do them."

"I'll help you, child," Filomena offered.

Linda put her hand on Filomena's cheek. *"Gracias,"* she said. "But you have been beaten. You should have rest. Manuel and I can take care of things. You will find him, won't you, John?"

"I'll find him," Slocum promised. "In the meantime, you get ready to leave. I'm going to take the two of you back to town. You'll be safe there."

"No," Linda insisted. "I'll stay here."

"I don't think that's such a good idea. Rawls and his bunch might come back."

"Why would they come back? There is nothing to come back for," Linda said. "Besides, I must see to the burial of my parents and my brother. And Filomena is in no condition to travel. The ride to town may be too much for her."

Slocum looked at Linda for a long moment. Something told him to force the issue, to make her return to town with him whether she wanted to or not. It wasn't just because he was concerned that Rawls might return. It was also because he didn't think he should leave her here in this place of death. She was calm now, but he knew it was a calm brought on by numbness, from having too much dropped on her too soon. When that numbness wore off, it wouldn't be good for her to be alone. And yet, even as he was thinking that, he was admiring her strength and determination. And he knew that in the same situation, no one could make him leave. Besides, she might be right about Filomena. The old woman was in pretty bad shape.

He sighed. "All right," he agreed reluctantly. "I'll leave you here for a while. In the meantime, while I'm looking for Bustamante, I'm going to check the place over, just to make certain none of Rawls's men are still here."

Slocum left the main house and started toward the outbuildings. Even before he reached the barn, he knew he was going to find something. By now the sun was high and hot, and he could smell the unmistakable stench of death.

He saw someone on the ground just outside the barn. When he walked closer, he recognized the man who had spoken to him the night before, with half a dozen bullet holes in him. Manuel was an old man, and he wasn't armed. He'd been shot down out of pure meanness. He couldn't have represented any threat to the robbers.

"*Amigo,* you had this all figured last night," Slocum said quietly to the body. "Too bad you didn't pay attention to your own instincts."

There were two more bodies inside the barn and a couple out in the corral. There was another draped across the corral fence, two more in the field beyond. The bodies lay bloating in the sun, and they were already beginning to ripen and attract the carrion-eating varmints. Vultures circled overhead, and some wild dogs were creeping down from the hills.

Slocum knew there was no way Linda could handle all this. She said she was going to oversee the burial of her parents, but who would she oversee? She was counting on Bustamante to help her, but he was dead and so was everyone else. There was no one even left to do the burying. The place looked like the aftermath of some of the battles Slocum had been in during the War.

There was only one thing to do now, Slocum decided,

and that was to ride over to the Delgado ranch. Whatever bad blood there may have been between Soltano and Delgado no longer existed. The war was over by virtue of the fact that Soltano and all his soldiers were dead. Delgado was the victor by default. Maybe he would be generous in his victory. Maybe he would send some of his people over to help Linda bury her dead.

Slocum worked for nearly half an hour to pull all the bodies into a pile just inside the barn. Once he had them in a pile he spread a tarpaulin over them. It was temporary at best, but at least it got the bodies out of the hot sun and, most importantly, out of Linda's sight should she happen to glance through the window. After Slocum finished with the dead, he went back inside and saw that Linda had put Filomena to bed and was stretched out on the bed beside her. Both women were sleeping. That was good. Linda needed the rest and if she could sleep for a while, it would keep her from wandering outside and happening on to the horror that waited for her there. Quietly, he slipped out of the house, then started the long ride toward Rancho Delgado.

At first it was pencil-thin and so light that he was able to convince himself that he was merely imagining things. But as he drew closer to the Delgado ranch, the column of smoke became more visible. When he was less than a mile away the smoke was roiling into the sky and a sickening spin of his stomach sent bile rising to his throat. Unless he badly missed his guess, Rawls had already been this way.

The fire was still snapping and popping when Slocum arrived, but there was very little left to burn. What had been the house was now a twisted mass of blackened timbers with just enough fuel left to support the dying flames. Here, as at the Soltano Rancho, men were lying about in pools of their own blood. One added element to the raid here was the number of slain horses. A dozen horses lay on the ground in the corral, like the men, victims of a senseless slaughter.

"Have you come to finish the job, *señor?*" a weak voice challenged.

Slocum heard the deadly click of a pistol being cocked, and he turned to see that one of the men had raised himself to his elbows. Slocum was looking down the barrel of a .45, though the man holding it was so weak that the gun was describing tiny circles. Slocum had never seen him, but the man fit the description of Delgado.

"You are Delgado?" Slocum asked.

"I am Delgado."

"Who did this?"

Delgado coughed, then laughed.

"That is a very funny joke, *señor.*" He wheezed and the gun dipped down. With strength gathered from somewhere deep inside, Delgado raised the gun again. "*Sí,* it is a very funny joke," he said. "You come and kill Delgado and all his men, then you ask who did this?"

"Look at me," Slocum said. "Look close. Am I one of them?"

Delgado tried to concentrate on Slocum's features with eyes that seemed to swim in their sockets. Finally, with a sigh, he lowered his gun, then lay back on the ground.

"You are not one of them, *señor,*" he agreed in a weak voice.

"Who was it?"

"It was Soltano's men—the six *gringos* he hired. You can tell Soltano he has won the war. All of my men are dead." Delgado sighed. "I am dead, *señor.* I am just waiting to close my eyes."

"Don Soltano hasn't won a damn thing," Slocum told him. "He's dead."

Delgado looked up, confused. "Dead?"

"The men who did this, the Americans led by a man named Dave Rawls, also killed Soltano. They killed him and his son, and every man on the ranch."

"So, Soltano was caught in his own evil. The chickens have come home to roost." Delgado laughed. "This is very funny. Do you not think this is funny, *señor?*" Delgado asked. "Soltano hires men to stop the war and they stop it by killing all of the warriors on both sides. I think that is a good way to stop the war. This is very funny, *señor*. Why do you not laugh?"

Slocum squatted down beside the old guerrilla chieftain. He poured water on his handkerchief, then wet Delgado's lips.

"Gracias," Delgado said. He coughed again and blood flecked out onto his chin. The light in his eyes began fading. Slocum knew he would die soon.

"Señor Delgado," Slocum said, taking the bullets from his pocket. He showed them to the dying man. "These bullets? Do you know anything about them? Do you know anyone who passes out such bullets?"

Delgado looked at the bullets, but already Slocum could see that he was drawing his final breaths.

"Do you know anything about them?" Slocum asked again.

Delgado shook his head, no, opened his mouth as if he were going to speak, then sucked in a last, desperate gasp of air. The air escaped from his throat in a long death rattle, then his head fell to one side. His eyes didn't close, but the light went out and they became opaque and unseeing. Delgado was dead.

Slocum stood up and sighed. He looked around the ranch, at the scattered bodies, the burning house, then suddenly his stomach started to churn again. If they burned this ranch, why didn't they also burn the Hacienda del Soltano? Perhaps they intended to. Perhaps his untimely arrival had sent them off to take care of Delgado. Now, with him over here, they could get back to what he had interrupted.

Slocum ran to his horse, mounted, and took off at a gallop for the Soltano ranch. As soon as he crested the range of hills which separated the two ranches, he saw a thick column of dark smoke rising like a spire into the sky. He bent low over his horse's neck and urged it to greater and still greater speed. He came onto the Soltano grounds at a full gallop. The bunkhouse, barn, and granary were ablaze, and he saw a man tossing a torch into the courtyard of the house.

"You house-burning son of a bitch!" Slocum shouted. He pulled his pistol and shot at the barn-burner, but the range was too great. He did get a pretty good look at the man, though, and saw that he wasn't an American but a short, swarthy Mexican who looked vaguely familiar.

Slocum swung down from his horse and ran to the house. He grabbed a couple of blankets, carried them back out to the well, soaked them in water, then returned to the house. With the wet blankets he was able to beat out the fire in the house before it got too much headway. He didn't even try to save the other buildings, which were roaring infernos. He remembered the bodies he had dragged into the barn. There would be no burial for them now. The fire had taken care of that.

Where was Linda? Why hadn't she come to help him fight the fire? Slocum, his face blackened with smoke, ran back into the house and began searching frantically for her.

"Linda! Linda!" he shouted. He ran into the bedroom where he had last seen her, then he stopped and put his hand on the door frame.

"Oh, shit," he said quietly. "Filomena, I'm sorry. I shouldn't have left the two of you. I should've stayed."

Filomena couldn't hear a word Slocum was saying. There was a fresh bullet hole in her chest and a pool of blood on the bed. Filomena was dead.

Linda was nowhere to be found.

11

Slocum had learned long ago to pay attention to hunches. His hunch had told him to take Linda and Filomena into town, but he had let himself be talked out of it. He should have stuck by his guns. If he had, Filomena would be alive and Linda would be safe. But it was too late now to be thinking about it. All he could do now was try to find Linda, and hope she was still safe.

For a moment Slocum considered hitting the trail, while the tracks of the murderers were still fresh. But he couldn't leave Linda's family scattered all over the house. He collected the bodies of Filomena, the don, his wife, and Joaquin, and put them all in the front room, where he covered them with sheets He hated to leave them like this, but he knew that the smoke from the burning buildings would draw others from town eventually and they would take care of the burial. He had no time to wait. Besides, nothing he could do would help Joaquin and the others, but if he acted quickly enough, Slocum could still help Linda. It was a matter of priority: help the living—it was too late for the dead. Linda was still alive, he felt, and he intended to keep her that way. Rawls had her, but Slocum would get her back.

When Slocum looked around outside, he saw several tracks coming to and from the ranch. Just by looking at them, he had no idea whether the tracks belonged to the outlaws or to some of the ranch hands who had run when the shooting started. He was certain that some of the hands had run, because he had found only eight bodies, and he knew that Soltano had a lot more hands riding for him than that.

Slocum had to be careful. If he followed the wrong set of tracks, it would throw him off for days. His best bet, he decided, would be to follow the set of tracks left by the Mexican who had come back to torch the buildings. He knew which tracks belonged to him, and the Mexican was sure to lead him to the others.

A short distance away from the main buildings of the rancho, Slocum figured he had made the right choice. The Mexican he trailed joined up with two other riders, and they cut a trail to the north. Slocum dismounted, then knelt on the trail to study the three sets of hoofprints.

The Mexican's hoofprints were easy to identify because of a bar in one of the shoes. Another set of hoofprints left a more shallow impression than the others, indicating that the horse was being ridden by a light rider. Slocum hoped it was Linda.

Linda sat on her horse looking at Dave Rawls. He was holding his hat in his hand, wiping his brow with a red bandanna. His hair was blond, his eyes so pale a blue as to be almost colorless. He had a scraggly growth of beard on his face, but it was so fine and so light in color that one had to look twice to see it.

"I don't know how the hell you goddamn greasers can live in this heat," he said nastily. "Jesus, it's hot."

"If you don't like it, you can always leave," Linda invited.

Rawls laughed. "Leave, yeah," he said. "Well, I tell you, honey, I intend to do just that. Only I'm takin' you with me." He laughed again.

"What do you intend to do with me?" Linda asked.

"Oh, don't you worry your pretty little head about that," Rawls told her, chuckling to himself. "I'll find somethin' to do with you." He laughed again. "Tell me about Slocum."

"What?" Linda asked, surprised by the question.

"John Slocum," Rawls repeated. "Tell me about him."

"He is . . . a good man," Linda said timidly.

"Is he fast?"

"Fast?"

"Yes, fast, damn it! Don't you understand a thing I'm saying to you? Is he fast with a gun?"

"I don't know," Linda answered honestly. "I've never seen him shoot a gun, nor have I heard him speak of it."

Rawls pulled his pistol for perhaps the hundredth time since Linda had been with him. He turned the cylinder to check the loads, then put the pistol back in his holster.

"I've heard he's fast," Rawls growled. "I've heard he's fast as greased lightnin'." Rawls smiled evilly, pulling his lips tight across his teeth. "I'm hopin' I get a chance to find that out. I reckon he'll be comin' after you . . . and when he does, me 'n' him's goin' to have a little face-to-face meetin', all fair and square."

"If that's true, why are you trying to ambush him?"

"Don't you worry about that ambush none, honey.

Unless I really miss my guess, Slocum ain't dumb enough to get caught in anything like that. No, ma'am, it's gonna come down to Slocum 'n' me."

"If he's as fast as you think, why would you want to face him? Aren't you afraid he might kill you?"

"They's always that chance, honey," Rawls agreed. "But iffen I kill him, I'll be known all over as the man that got Slocum. That'd be a good reputation for a man in my profession to carry 'round with 'im."

"Profession? What kind of profession do you have besides murder and robbery?" Linda asked sharply.

"I'm a professional shootist," Rawls said proudly. "Them other things, the murder and robbery, why, they just sort of go with the territory, that's all."

All the while Rawls talked, Linda was working on part of her dress, rubbing it against a rough corner on her saddle pommel. Now, at last, she had the dress shredded so she could tear off little pieces one at a time. She dropped a piece on the ground, then started preparing the next piece.

"Come on," Rawls said, putting his hat back on his head. "No sense in us just sitting here waiting for him. The least I can do is make him come to us. Besides, we'll be meeting the boys in another few minutes."

They rode on again, and Linda dropped another little piece of black cloth.

Please, dear God, she prayed silently. *Let John Slocum see the trail I'm leaving for him. Let him find me and rescue me from this man.*

Slocum got on his horse again and started following the three sets of tracks. After about a quarter of a mile the Mexican's tracks veered off. Slocum followed them for several yards, then realized what it meant. The Mexican had circled round, intending to come up on his backtrail.

Slocum patted the neck of his horse, then stood in his stirrups and looked back along the trail he had just ridden. He couldn't see anyone, but he knew the Mexican was back there.

"Well, boy, what do you think?" Slocum asked his horse. "Should I stay here and gutshoot that barn-burning son of a bitch? Or should I follow the other set of tracks?"

Even as Slocum was asking the question aloud, a small piece of black cloth caught his eye. He got off his horse, walked over, and picked it up. He examined it closely for a few seconds, then smiled.

"Well, well, what do you think of this?" he asked his horse.

The cloth he found was a scrap of Linda's black dress. He remounted, following the tracks a while longer, and found another piece of black cloth. They were small, difficult to see, but Slocum realized that Linda was tearing them off and dropping them on the ground for his benefit.

The question he had posed a moment earlier was answered. He would follow Linda, get ahead of the Mexican. Slocum spurred his horse along the trail left by Linda. He realized quickly that the men who had taken her were heading toward Santa Luz, and he hoped they would wind up there. He believed it would be easier to find them, call them out, in town.

A short while later his hopes of catching up easily were dashed, when the tracks he was following joined up with others. Here, Slocum realized, the gang had switched mounts. Their horses were fresh now, while his was tired. That meant they would outdistance him quite easily, and even if he got to within closing distance, they could outrun him. To make things worse, Slocum also noticed that the tracks were no longer headed for Santa Luz, but were going north toward the border.

"Shit!" he said aloud. He knew that, for the moment at least, he would have to abandon the trail. Dejectedly, he continued on toward Santa Luz.

Word of the massacres at the Soltano and Delgado ranchos had already reached Santa Luz by the time Slocum rode into town. Delgado had more friends in town than Soltano, but some of the men who rode for Soltano—the old ones who had worked for Soltano's father before him—were also liked. And, given that the disaster had struck both ranches without distinction, the supporters of both factions had put their differences aside in their mutual shock over what had happened. Men who but a few days before had been bitter enemies were now allied in their grief. Riders from both ranches who had been spared in the massacre were now sharing whiskey in the cantina.

Slocum went into the cantina and ordered a drink. He looked round the place and recognized three or four men he knew to be riders for Soltano.

"Where were you when the shooting started?" he asked accusingly.

"*Señor,* the men who did this, the *gringos,* are not human. They are devils!" one of the riders explained for all of them.

"Of course they're human," Slocum growled. "They're men, just like you and me. If a few of you had had the guts to stand up to them, none of this would have happened."

"You did not see them, *señor.* They were like madmen, killing and laughing and killing some more."

"God damn it! There were only six of them," Slocum swore gruffly. "There must've been two dozen or more of you. Why didn't you fight them off?"

"We are workers, *señor,* not soldiers."

"Seems to me like you were lording it up pretty good when you were running over the smaller ranchers around here," Slocum said accusingly. He looked at the Delgado riders as well as the Soltano riders. "All of you were riding high a few days ago. Now that you've found someone who could shoot back, you suddenly turned yellow."

"If we had not run, *señor,* we would have been dead now."

"*Si,* we would all be dead too," a Delgado man agreed.

"Why do you speak to us of fighting?" one of the Soltano riders asked. "Are you not one of the *gringos* Don Soltano hired to fight for him? Where were you, *señor,* when all this happened? Maybe if you had been with the *gringos* they would not have done such a terrible thing."

"I was not hired by Soltano to fight," Slocum said firmly. "I brought him horses, that's all. But tell me, if the *gringos* had killed only Delgado men instead of Soltano and Delgado men, would you still think it was a terrible thing?"

"*Si señor.* Of course. To kill many people is a terrible thing."

"They were hired to kill Delgado and his men," Slocum said. "The only thing that went wrong is they got a little out of hand, that's all. If it had been just Delgado and his men who died, none of you Soltano bunch would've said a word."

Slocum regretted saying this almost as soon as the words were out of his mouth. The first overtures of reconciliation were already being sowed and he had nearly disrupted it with his frank words. He figured it was time to change the subject.

"They've got Soltano's daughter with them," Slocum told them. "I'm going after her."

"I wish you luck, *señor,*" one of the men said.

"There are some people who need buryin'," Slocum went on. "At both ranches. Since there's no danger left from the outlaws, maybe some of you would take care of it."

"*Si, señor,*" said the man who had wished him luck. "Do not worry. We will give them all a fine burial."

"*Gracias,*" Slocum replied. He tossed down his drink, then left the cantina to go back to his hotel room. He intended to get his things, check out of the hotel, and immediately go back on the trail after Rawls. But Angelina was in the lobby of the hotel when Slocum stepped inside.

"John," Angelina said, smiling as she saw him. "I am glad you are still here. I thought you were gone."

"I soon will be," Slocum informed her. "As soon as I can get my bedroll and clothes together, buy a few provisions, and fill up my canteens."

"I have heard of the killings at the Soltano and Delgado ranchos," Angelina said. "It is a terrible thing."

"Yeah," Slocum agreed. "Did you hear about Linda?"

"The daughter of Soltano? No, I have heard nothing. Was she killed?"

"No, but they've got her with them."

"Who?"

"Rawls," Slocum said. "Rawls and the other Americans. And the Mexican."

"The Mexican? What Mexican?" Angelina asked. "I thought the ones who did all this were Americans."

"I did too, at first," Slocum said. "But when I rode back into the courtyard of the Hacienda del Soltano today, I saw a Mexican trying to burn the place. I took a shot at him, but I missed."

"Who was it?"

"I don't know," Slocum said. "But I have the feeling I've seen him before. Anyway, whoever he is, he's mixed up with the Americans. I tracked him until I found where he had joined up with the others."

"What did they do with Linda Soltano?"

"She's with them," Slocum answered. "They picked up fresh mounts, then the tracks turned north. My horse was too tired to go on, but I'm going back after them now. I'm going after them and I'm going to find them. You can count on that."

"They are bad men, John. There will be great danger for you if you go after them."

"I'm not telling myself it'll be easy. But I can't just leave Linda to them," Slocum explained. "I don't know what they have in mind for her, but I can guess."

Slocum put his hand down in his pocket and pulled out the two bullets, the one which had been thrown into his room and the other, which he found on the floor by the don's body. He showed the bullets to Angelina.

"These two bullets were left for me. Both of them carry my name. Ever seen anything like this before? Do they mean anything to you?"

Angelina turned pale.

"What is it? What does it mean?" Slocum asked, noticing her reaction.

"This has happened before," she told him. "When Don Eduardo was acquiring land. The small landowners who refused him got a bullet like these. The next day, they were dead."

"Soltano did it?"

"Maybe," Angelina answered slowly. "I do not know. Maybe someone else."

What was it? Slocum wondered to himself. What was going on? Something important clawed at his mind, trying to form, but it wouldn't come. It was like trying to pick up quicksilver. He just couldn't grab hold.

12

Slocum was coming out the front door of the hotel, carrying his saddlebags across his shoulder, when a woman approached him carrying a bundle.

"*Señor* Slocum?"

Slocum stopped and looked at her. She held the bundle out toward him. At first he was puzzled, then he realized what it was. His clothes, the clothes Linda had taken the night before to have cleaned.

"These, the *señorita* gave to me last night," she said. "I have washed them for you."

"Yeah, I almost forgot about those," Slocum told her.

He reached into his pocket for money, but the woman stopped him with a wave of her hand. "They are paid for."

"*Gracias,*" Slocum said. He took the bundle from the woman, saw a cloth tobacco sack on top of the bundle.

"What's this?" he asked. The old woman shook her

head, then turned and started walking quickly away.

Curious, he opened the sack. A bullet fell out. Like the other two, a .45 caliber.

Slocum held the bullet up and examined the soft lead of the slug. There, scratched in the lead, was his name. This time, there was one other word. *"Pronto."*

Soon.

"Señora!" Slocum called out. *"Señora,* wait!"

The woman stopped and looked around.

"Where did you get this tobacco sack?"

"Que dice?" the woman asked in confusion.

"The tobacco sack," Slocum yelled to her, holding the bag out in front of him. "Where did you get it?" He held the bullet up as well. "What about this bullet? Do you know anything about it?"

The woman looked at the bullet and her eyes grew wide with fright. She shook her head, then turned and began running.

"Wait a minute, damn it!" Slocum called. For a moment, he considered running after her, but decided against it. Maybe she really didn't know. Or maybe she did know and was terrified to say anything about it. It could be that she was being watched, right now, by whoever put the bag in the bundle. And if that was the case, he was being watched as well.

Slocum looked up and down the street and across the plaza of the little town. A pall of dust hung in the air and, farther out, heat waves shimmered under the hot sun. He didn't see anyone, but he felt odd, as if someone was watching him at that very moment. It was more than a hunch. He had felt this way before. He knew, without knowing why. And whoever it was was close by. It was somebody who knew he would come to town. Someone either waiting or following him. Slocum speculated that it could be the Mexican he saw riding away from the hacienda. The man had doubled back on Slocum's trail once; maybe he did it again. The thing that was in Slocum's mind began to crawl out of the black depths of memory. But he couldn't put a finger to it, or a name.

Slocum dropped this bullet into his pocket with the others, then he pulled out the makings for a cigarette. He stuffed it loosely between his lips, lit it, and clamped it between his teeth as he climbed onto his horse.

The shot came just as he was leaving town. The crack of the rifle and the deadly whine of lead searing the air reached his ears simultaneously. Only luck saved him. He had hunched in the saddle for a moment to adjust his rump against the cantle just as the shot was fired. The bullet whizzed by right where his head had been an instant before.

Slocum saw a puff of white smoke hanging in the air two hundred yards away. He spit out his smoke, flattened against his horse, kicked it into a gallop, and rode in a zigzag pattern toward the knoll below the little cloud of smoke. He drew his pistol and pointed it toward the spot just under the smoke. If so much as a hair showed above the crest, he would blast it. He covered the two hundred yards in about fifteen seconds, charged around the knoll, then jumped from the saddle and rolled on the ground toward the cover of a nearby rock.

There was no one there.

Slocum lay behind the rock for a long moment until he was absolutely certain that he was alone. Then he moved cautiously over to where his ambusher had waited for him. On the ground was the spent cartridge of a .44–40 jacked out of a Winchester by the assailant after firing. There were horse tracks nearby and, when Slocum examined them, he saw that the hoofprints were the bar-

shoe tracks of the Mexican who had set fire to the buildings at the Soltano ranch.

"So, my friend, you are still with me, are you?" Slocum
said to himself. He smiled. "Good. That'll help me pick
up the trail again."

Slocum swung back onto his horse and followed the
Mexican's tracks out of town. The Mexican knew he was
being tracked, and he did everything he could to throw
Slocum off. He rode across solid rock; he tied brush to
his horse's tail to drag out tracks; he cut and re-cut his
own trail. Grim-faced, Slocum hung on doggedly, his
mind ranging over his options. He did not want to make
a mistake, not now. Linda's life might depend on his
decision.

Slocum could have overtaken the Mexican and had it
out with him then and there. He held back, though,
believing that, despite the Mexican's attempts to confuse
him, he would eventually lead him to the others . . . and
to Linda. When darkness fell that night, Slocum saw the
Mexican's campfire. He was pretty sure that it was a
false campfire, set by the Mexican in hope of luring
Slocum into an early camp. Slocum moved cautiously
through the night until he reached the Mexican's fire. He
looked around and saw that he had been right. The Mexican hadn't camped at that spot and had no intention of
camping there.

Slocum continued until he came to a range of steep,
rocky hills. He was certain the Mexican wouldn't try
these in the dark and, even if he did, Slocum wouldn't
be able to follow his tracks. He decided that it was best
to stop and wait for the light of day.

From the position of the stars, Slocum supposed that it
was about two in the morning. He had been sleeping,

but something woke him up. He lay quietly for a few minutes, listening to the sounds in the night. Wind sighed through the dry limbs of a nearby mesquite tree, his horse whickered, but everything else was silent. Still, something had awakened him.

Quietly, Slocum rolled away from his sleeping bag. He crawled over to a small depression, slipped down into it, and looked back at his bedroll. From his position, it looked like someone was still in the blankets.

There was a sudden flash of flame from a muzzle-blast and the crack of a rifle shot. A puff of dust flew up from the bedroll. Slocum realized that if he had still been there, he would be dead now.

Slocum waited to see if his nocturnal assailant would follow up his ambush. There were no more shots and no one appeared. A moment later Slocum heard the sound of hoofbeats drumming against the hard, rocky ground. The Mexican, if that was who it was, had made a hasty retreat without checking to see whether he had killed Slocum or not.

Slocum let him get away. If the Mexican thought Slocum was dead, he might be less cautious, and the trail would be easier to follow.

His hunch was right. The Mexican did get a bit more careless. Slocum picked up the trail quite easily the next day, and he smiled broadly when he saw that the Mexican had rejoined the others. From the number of tracks he counted, Slocum was sure that the outlaws were driving a remuda, and because the drive was slowing them down, he began gaining on them. Soon, he believed, he would overtake them.

That belief was scuttled, however, when he came upon several abandoned horses. The outlaws and Linda had switched to the purebreds and let their old horses go. With fresh mounts—mounts of the quality Slocum had brought down from Texas—they would soon open up a great distance between them and Slocum.

Slocum dismounted and walked toward the tiredly grazing horses. One of them whickered and stamped his foot, and Slocum was afraid they would all be spooked.

"Easy, fella," he said. "Just take it easy now."

Slocum approached, talking quietly. He reached out and patted the horse on the neck. The horse stood still and the others calmed down.

Slocum looked on the horse's flank and saw an R-S brand. "Don't know that one," he said aloud. He looked at the other brands, recognized none of them until the last one he checked. It carried the humpbacked "S" of the Soltano ranch.

"So," Slocum said aloud. "Now I know who the enemy is. I know who he has been all along."

Slocum remounted his own horse, took a drink of water, and wiped his mouth with the back of his hand. Maybe Rawls had gained a temporary advantage by changing to the purebreds. But that advantage would be wiped out by a big mistake Rawls had made. Slocum had never seen Dave Rawls, and he didn't know the faces of any of the American outlaws. He could have run into one of them in broad daylight and not known him. That might have presented a problem, especially if he encountered them in a village. But, thanks to Rawls, that problem was now solved.

Slocum didn't know the riders, but he certainly knew their horses. He had picked them out, one by one, and trailed them all the way to Mexico. He could recognize one of them from four hundred yards away. And he did know the Mexican on sight. He was going to lose some time catching up to the fresh mounts, but it was well worth the trade.

Slocum smiled, then resumed his chase. The tracks ran together for about another mile, then split into two groups. Slocum followed one of the groups. As he did so, it gradually reduced in size, one rider at a time, until after fifteen miles he was down to a pair of tracks.

He stopped as the last two riders separated and looked back over the trail.

Maybe he should have stayed with the other group when the riders separated for the first time. But he had chosen the largest group. Now, if he backtracked to pick up the other group, he would lose at least a day. Not only that, there was no guarantee that it wouldn't do the same thing this group did, decrease by one rider at a time until he was left with only one man to track.

Slocum drew a deep breath and made his decision. If there was only one man to follow, he didn't intend to let that man get away from him. Right now, that man, whoever he was, was Slocum's only connection with Linda. He slapped his legs against the side of his horse and urged him on.

"Let's go," he said in a determined voice. "I've got a few questions I want to ask this fella, whoever the hell he is."

Slocum followed the trail for another five miles. Then, in the distance before him, sending up heat waves under the punishing sun, he spotted a small village.

Slocum knew the town. It was Paso Corto, and he had passed through it on his way down to deliver the horses. He had thought then that when he came back through he would have his pockets full of money.

Slocum climbed off his horse and led it over to a clump of trees. He took off the saddle.

"Might as well let you be comfortable for a while," he said to the grateful animal. "I'm going to wait for nightfall before I take a look around down there."

Slocum dropped his saddle in the shade of a tree and lay down to wait for darkness. Having slept little, and fitfully, the night before, Slocum had no problem napping through the long afternoon.

His dreams, full of horses and the blank faces of hard men, left him drenched with the sweat of a powerful worry.

13

The night creatures called to each other as Slocum stood looking toward Paso Corto. The cloud passed over the moon and moved away, bathing in silver the little town that rose up like a ghost before him. A couple of dozen adobe buildings, half of which were lit up, fronted the town plaza. The biggest and most brightly lit building was the lone cantina at the far end of town.

Inside the cantina someone was playing a guitar, and Slocum could hear the music all the way out in the hills. The player was good, and the music spilled out a steady beat with two or three poignant minor chords at the end of each phrase. An overall, single string melody worked its way in and out of the chords like a thread of gold woven through the finest cloth. Slocum liked that kind of music, mournful, lonesome music, the kind of melody a man could let run through his mind during long, quiet rides.

Slocum saddled his horse but decided to put on a hobble and walk into town. He didn't particularly want to be seen and he decided his arrival would be less noticeable if he arrived on foot. He checked his pistols. They were loaded and slipped easily from their sheaths. From the insight of years on the trail, nurtured by the need of living by his wits, he knew he would soon be using these guns. In an arena where two gunfighters, both quick as thought, would be going against each other, victory often came to the man, not always the fastest, who had the edge. Slocum's edge was that he knew one of the men he was looking for was in this town . . . but the man didn't know that Slocum was coming.

Slocum started into town, caught the smell of beans and spicy beef from one of the houses, and realized that it had been a couple of days since he had eaten well. His stomach growled in protest.

A dog barked, a ribbony yap that was silenced by a kick or a thrown rock.

A baby cried, a sudden gargle that cracked the air like a bullwhip.

A housewife raised her voice in one of the houses, launching into some private tirade about something, sharing her anger with all who were within earshot.

Though normally Slocum walked down the middle of a street to avoid ambush from the shadows, this was an entirely different situation. This time the shadows, instead of being his enemy, were his ally. He moved through them, staying out of sight until he reached the cantina. There, in the lantern light which spilled through the door, he saw one of the purebreds he had brought down from Texas. It stood hipshot at the burro-high hitchrail out front.

Slocum listened to the sounds from the cantina. The music had stopped and now there was only conversation, Mexican mostly, but he froze when he heard the unmistakable accent of an American ordering *"un otra copa."*

Slocum looked up and down the street to make certain no one watched the cantina door. The he stepped up onto the board porch and pushed his way inside. He pulled his hatbrim low and headed for the bar, positioning himself in a way that put his back to the wall. He glanced across the room and spied the American in a far corner, an empty plate in front of the man, a pistol beside it on the table.

Slocum studied the American for a moment before the other man even noticed him. Medium height, very thin, with a thick moustache under a rather large nose. His face was pockmarked, his hair a dirty blond. Slocum knew this had to be the man he had followed all day.

"Que quieres?" the bartender asked.

The owlhoot looked up when the bartender spoke to Slocum, and his eyes registered surprise at seeing another American in the cantina. The surprise was quickly replaced by recognition, though, when the man suddenly realized who Slocum must be and began to study him cautiously.

"Give me a shot of tequila," Slocum ordered in English.

The bartender reached for a bottle and a glass, then poured the drink. He slid the glass across the bar to Slocum.

"Dos pesos, señor," he said, holding up two fingers.

Slocum started to reach for his money. Then, out of the corner of his eye, he saw that the border jumper at the table was standing up with his pistol in his hand.

Slocum slipped his own pistol out quick as a snake, and he and the other American stood facing each other, pistols drawn.

"You can talk or you can die," Slocum said quietly. He didn't have to speak loud, because every voice in the cantina fell silent when the men faced each other over drawn guns.

"Fuck you, Slocum," the American rasped.

The quiet room was shattered with the roar of two pistols exploding. The Mexicans yelled and dived or scrambled for cover. White gunsmoke billowed out in a cloud that filled the center of the room, momentarily obscuring everything.

As the smoke began to clear, the outlaw stared through the white cloud, smiling broadly at Slocum. He opened his mouth as if to speak. The only sound he made, however, was a gagging rattle way back in his throat. The smile left his face, his eyes glazed over, and he pitched forward, his gun clattering to the floor.

Slocum stood ready to fire a second shot if needed, but a second shot wasn't necessary. He looked down at the dead American for a moment, then holstered his pistol. He picked up the gun the outlaw used and examined it—a converted Remington .44, the nipples bored out to accept brass cartridges. The bullets did not match the slugs in his pocket that someone had sent him as a warning.

"Anybody know his name?" Slocum asked. He looked around the cantina, studying every face. All heads were shaking, and he didn't see an expression of recognition in any of them. He also did not see the Mexican he had been following.

"When did he get here?" Slocum asked, pointing to the dead American on the floor.

"Today, *señor,*" the bartender answered. "He came this afternoon, ate his dinner, and drank. He spoke to no one."

If the man had arrived that same afternoon, Slocum reasoned, he was definitely the one he'd been tracking. Besides, the outlaw knew Slocum's name. That meant he had to be one of the six Americans hired by Soltano.

All right, Slocum thought. *That's one down and five to go.*

Slocum searched through the outlaw's pockets and found a hundred dollars in green. He put the money in his own pocket, then returned to the bar and tossed down the tequila he'd already paid for. At the other end of the bar, Slocum noticed a young boy, perhaps twelve years old.

"Boy," he called, pulling out a couple of pesos. "You know the stand of alamo trees just south of town?"

"Si," the boy said.

Slocum tossed the money to him. "You'll find my horse there. Bring him into town."

The boy took the money and scooted out the front door.

"There a hotel in this town?"

"Next door," the bartender answered.

"When the boy gets back with my horse, tell him where I am. Tell him to stable the horse."

Slocum took out ten dollars and set it on the bar, then looked at the body of the outlaw he had just killed.

"Bury him deep," he said.

"Si, señor," the bartender said, picking up the money.

There was a cafe in the front of the hotel and Slocum sat down with his back to the wall and facing the door. He ordered a meal of chili, steak, tortillas, and coffee. The boy came in before he was finished eating.

"I put up your horse, *señor.*"

"Gracias," Slocum said, taking out a few more pesos.

"Was he a bad man? The one you killed?"

"Yes," Slocum stated firmly.

The boy smiled. "I thought he was. I could tell when he came to town today that he was a bad man."

"How could you tell?"

"His eyes," the boy said, moving his fingers across his own eyes. "They were evil. His smile was not happy. He drank much, and he watched the door. I believe he was looking for you, *señor.*"

"Yes," Slocum agreed. "He was."

"Did he rob a bank?"

"I don't know."

"If you don't know, why did you hunt for him?"

"He killed some friends of mine, and he and some other bad men took a girl captive. I was following them but they split up. I kept on the trail until I found him here. I don't know where the others are."

"Duermequi," the boy said.

"What?"

"He asked how far to Duermequi. He said he had to meet someone there. Maybe it is the other bad men and the girl."

Slocum smiled. "Maybe you're right," he said. He saw the boy watching him eat.

"Tell you what," Slocum offered. "I'm still a little hungry. If I ordered a plate of tamales and couldn't eat them all, could you help me?"

The boy's face lit up in a smile. *"Si, señor,"* he answered.

Slocum ordered, and a few moments later a plate of tamales was set on the table. He took one, then slid the plate toward the boy.

"You only want one?"

"Yeah," Slocum said. "They're good, but I guess I'm not as hungry as I thought."

"Gracias," the boy said to Slocum, as he slipped one of the spicy cylinders of ground meat out of its cornhusk wrapping and began to eat happily.

Slocum was behind a plow on his father's farm in Georgia. The sun was low and the furrows, long and straight, were fire-red in the sun's glow. Slocum had never seen ground so red. It blazed up at him with the deep crimson of blood. The earth was spread with blood. Rivers of it ran through the furrow, flooded around his feet, dripped from his plow.

"Señor!"

The warning cry cut through the layers of sleep as quickly as a knife through hot butter. The dream fell away, and Slocum, with reflexes born of years of living on the edge, rolled off the bed just as a gun boomed in the doorway of his room. The bullet slammed into the headboard of the bed where, a second earlier, Slocum had been sleeping.

At the same time Slocum rolled off the bed, he grabbed the pistol from under his pillow. Now the advantage was his. The man who attempted to kill him was temporarily blinded by the muzzle flash of his own shot and he could see nothing in the darkness of Slocum's room. That same muzzle flash, however, had illuminated the assailant for Slocum and he quickly aimed his pistol at the dark hulk in the doorway, closed his eyes against his own muzzle flash, and squeezed the trigger. The gun bucked in his hand as the roar filled the room.

To Slocum there was a measurable amount of time between the explosion of the intruder's gun and his own.

To others in the hotel, or in the nearby buildings, however, the two shots came so close together as to be almost simultaneous. In a little village like Paso Corto, drunken patrons of the cantina often vented their spirit with the discharge of pistols. But the villagers had learned to recognize the difference in sound of shots fired in play and those fired in anger. Everyone within hearing knew that these were angry shots. A few of the more pious crossed themselves as they realized that someone had just died.

Slocum heard a groaning sound, then the heavy thump of a falling body.

"*Señor? Senor*, are you killed?" the Mexican boy asked in a frightened voice.

"No," Slocum answered. He struck a match, lit the candle lamp on the bedside table, then looked at the man he had just shot. The boy came into the room, stepping gingerly around the body.

"*Ay*, such shooting to kill him in the dark," the boy said.

"Yeah, well, the best shot in the world wouldn't have had a chance if he was asleep. He would've killed me if you hadn't shouted a warning, woke me up," Slocum said. "How'd you happen to be here?"

"After I ate the tamales, I went back to the cantina to sweep the floors," the boy explained. "This is my job. While I was working, this *gringo* came in, asked about his friend. When he learned his friend was dead, I knew he would try to kill you too, so I watched him all night. When he came to the hotel, I followed him. When I saw him come to your room, I yelled at you."

"And saved my life," Slocum said. He reached out and rubbed the boy's hair. "Thanks, friend. Thanks a lot."

The boy beamed under Slocum's gratitude.

Slocum examined the gun of the man who had attacked him. It was a Smith & Wesson .38. He shook his head in disappointment. This wasn't the man who was sending him bullets either. That man, whoever he was, was still out there somewhere, still waiting for him.

Slocum realized now that he was up against a determined bunch of men who intended to kill him. If it hadn't been for the Mexican boy, they would have succeeded. He would have to be more careful from now on.

A hell of a lot more careful.

14

Slocum left town before dawn, and by mid-morning now, the sun was a quarter of the way through its daily transit. Already the heat was fierce, and what little wind did stir blew against his face like a breath from the mouth of a blast furnace.

Ahead of him the brown land lay in empty folds of rocks, dirt, and cactus. The sun heated the ground, then sent up undulating waves which caused near objects to shimmer and nonexistent lakes to appear tantalizingly in the distance.

Slocum picked up the tracks of three riders. The ground was hard, and the tracks so indistinct that he could tell very little about them. He didn't know if Linda was one of the riders or not.

Often, Slocum would have to get down and examine the tracks very closely to make certain he was still on the right trail. That necessity saved his life, for just as he was dismounting, a rifle cracked and the bullet sizzled by, taking his hat off, fluffing his hair, and sending shivers down his spine.

In one motion, Slocum was on the ground and had the pistol out of his holster. He slapped his horse's flank to get him out of the line of fire, then dived for a nearby rock, just as a second shot came so close to his ear that he could hear the air pop as the bullet sped by.

Slocum wriggled his body under cover, then raised himself slowly and looked over the top of the rock. He couldn't see anyone, but he did see a little puff of white smoke drifting slowly to the east. That meant the shooter had to be somewhat west of the smoke. Slocum shifted his eyes in that direction. He saw a hat rise slowly above the rocks.

Slocum waited until he thought enough of the hat was visible to provide a target, then he shot. The hat went sailing away.

"You just put a hole in a twenty-dollar hat, you son of a bitch!" a voice called out. The voice was American.

"Sorry," Slocum called back. "I meant to put the hole in your head."

The marksman fired again and surprised Slocum, because he had his eyes fixed right where he thought the man would have to come up. Somehow the man had managed to slip down the rock for a small distance.

This bullet was as close as the first one. It hit the rock right in front of Slocum. It kicked tiny pieces of rock and shreds of hot lead into his face before it whined away behind him. Slocum turned around and slid down to the ground, brushing the hot lead from his cheeks.

"That is you, ain't it, Slocum?" the voice called. "I wouldn't want to go killin' the wrong fella."

"Are you Rawls?"

"Naw," the man answered. "Rawls, he's got the girl. He left me behind to take care of you. My name's Payson but some folks call me Fast Johnny. I reckon you've heard of me?"

"No, can't say as I have."

In fact, Slocum had heard of Fast Johnny Payson, a young gunman trying to make a name for himself. Slocum had heard that Payson had shot down a couple of well-known gunfighters who had all but retired because of age. Among those who didn't know better, the names of Fast Johnny's victims gave Fast Johnny the reputation he so eagerly sought. But those who really knew, knew that it was a cheap reputation.

"Are you shittin' me, Slocum? You really never heard of me?" Fast Johnny asked, obviously disappointed by Slocum's reply.

"Am I supposed to have heard of you?"

"You heard of Clay Temple, ain't you? And Honor Morgan?"

"I heard some punk kid dry-gulched them," Slocum answered coldly. "Never heard the punk's name."

"Folks'll hear it after it gets out I killed you," Fast Johnny yelled boldly.

"Want to step out from behind that rock and face me down?" Slocum challenged.

"All right," Fast Johnny called back. "I'll try you."

Slocum looked around the rock and saw that Fast Johnny was coming out from behind his cover with his pistols holstered and his hands spread out beside him. Slocum holstered his own pistol, then stood up.

"Well, I must confess you surprise me," Slocum told him. "I didn't think you'd do it."

"Maybe I got another surprise for you," Fast Johnny said, grinning evilly.

"You never can tell," Slocum replied. "You might..." Slocum's reply was interrupted by a pistol shot from off to his left. The bullet missed, though he didn't know how it could have, because he was so close to his assailant that Slocum felt the sting of burnt gunpowder.

"Billy, you dumb son of a bitch, you missed!" Fast Johnny cried as he went for his own gun.

Slocum had a fifth of a second to make a decision. Should he fire his first shot at Fast Johnny, who was just now going for his gun, or at Billy, who was now rising up from behind a nearby rock with his gun already in his hand?

Slocum decided to go for Payson. He'd heard tell of Fast Johnny's shooting—knew he was good. Billy had demonstrated his inaccuracy in the missed opportunity an instant earlier.

Quick as thought, Slocum's gun was cocked and booming. The bullet slammed into Fast Johnny's chest, severing arteries and tearing away vital heart tissue. Fast Johnny completed his draw and pulled the trigger, but he was already dead by the time his gun cleared his holster.

Before Fast Johnny fell, Slocum turned to fire at the other man, who was also firing. Billy's second shot proved as ineffective as his first, but Slocum's bullet hit Billy in the hip, causing him to double over and then crumple down in pain.

Slocum stood quietly for a moment as the echoes of the shots came rolling back from a nearby rock wall. When the last echo was a subdued rumble off a distant hill, the silence of the desert returned. The limbs of a nearby ocotillo rattled in the breeze. A shock of tumbleweed bounced by. A lizard scurried across a rock.

"Oh," Billy moaned. "Oh, son of a bitch, it hurts. Jesus, I've never had anything hurt like this."

"Where's Rawls?" Slocum asked. "The girl?"

"I'm gutshot," Billy cried out.

Slocum looked at the wound. It was in the hip, painful, but probably not fatal.

"You aren't gutshot."

"I'm gonna die."

"You won't die," Slocum said, "unless I kill you. Now where's Rawls?"

"I can't tell you that," Billy moaned.

"Have it your own way," Slocum said calmly. He held the pistol down toward Billy's head and cocked it. The cylinder turned with a metallic click, lining up the next cartridge under the hammer and firing pin.

"Are you . . . are you gonna kill me?"

"Looks like it," Slocum said.

"No, wait!" Billy shouted. "Don't kill me."

"Where's the girl?" Slocum asked again.

"Look, you gotta understand, this . . . all this ambush business, this wasn't my idea," Billy explained in desperation. "It was Fast Johnny's notion. He wanted to kill you, make a name for hisself. I just wanted to give you the message, like Rawls said."

"Message? What message?" Slocum asked.

"Rawls'll make you a trade, Slocum," Billy offered. "Rawls will give you the girl if you promise to back off. He knows everything you done."

"How?"

"You got a man on your backtrail and he picks up a fresh mount in every town, meets us at spots we set."

By now Billy had realized that the wound wasn't fatal, and he began to show a little more spirit.

"Then this was planned out pretty good, a long time ago," Slocum said. It wasn't a question.

"Yep."

"Why?"

Billy laughed. "Because Soltano had 'most a hundred thousand in that safe, and Delgado was good for another ten thousand."

"You must have an inside man."

"Two."

"Two?" Slocum was surprised by that.

Billy laughed. "Yeah, two. Ain't that the shits? That goes to show that you can't trust a damn Mex. Now, how about it, Slocum? What do I tell Rawls? Do we trade or not?"

"Rawls wants to buy me off with the girl? No cash?"

"That's right."

Slocum looked at Billy, who was now packing his wound with crushed leaves from a calliandra bush. Something was wrong here, but Slocum couldn't put his finger on it. Why had Rawls taken Linda in the first place? He had murdered everyone else. She must be slowing him down. Now he wanted to trade her so Slocum would stop hunting him. It didn't make sense to John Slocum.

"Well, what's your answer, Slocum?"

"Suppose you just tell Rawls to go to hell."

"I'll see to it he gets the message," Billy said. He stood up. The calliandra leaves were having a numbing effect on his pain, and now he was almost cocky. Slocum knew that the numbness would wear off and the pain would return, worse than before, but he said nothing. Billy limped over to the rock behind Fast Johnny's body.

There were two horses tied there. He climbed on one and took the reins of the other, then looked down at Slocum.

"One other thing," Billy went on. "You give me an hour's start. If you don't, the girl's dead . . . wolf meat, you savvy?"

"Yeah," Slocum growled. "I savvy."

Billy laughed. "You're lucky I wasn't killed like Fast Johnny here. If neither of us woulda come back, Rawls would kill her sure as hell. This way, if you behave yourself, I can tell Rawls what happened . . . tell him it wasn't your fault. That way he'll go easy on the girl till you change your mind and trade for her."

Slocum watched Billy ride away, then he walked over to look down at Fast Johnny's body. Fast Johnny was slack-jawed and hollow-eyed in death. The expression of surprise was frozen on his face, and a little dribble of blood oozed from his mouth. The insects were the early scavengers, and they were already crawling around on the body, staking their claim.

Slocum didn't particularly like to look at the men he killed. Except for the War, he had never killed a man unless it was absolutely necessary. During the War his officers told him who to kill, when to kill, how to kill. He was a sharpshooter, then, and he could kill a man at eight hundred yards. Of course, he didn't have to look at the men he killed. He could barely see them, and they never saw him. He didn't like to be told who to kill. That was why he never wore a badge. A lawman was like a soldier in that respect. If you wore a badge you were killing for someone else.

Slocum decided to bury Fast Johnny while he waited for Billy to clear out. He dragged the body over to a

small ravine and pushed it in, rolling it down the incline.
He started to throw the rocks down on the body, then he
happened to think that he should probably go through
the man's pockets for a clue as to where Rawls might
have Linda. He slid into the ravine, knelt down, and ran
his hand through Fast Johnny's pockets.

Slocum pulled an envelope from the dead man's shirt.
As he opened the envelope, a newspaper clipping fluttered out. The headline caught Slocum's attention:

DUEL ON FRONT STREET
CLAY TEMPLE KILLED
Famous gunman shot down by man named Payson

Slocum chuckled. Fast Johnny Payson carried around
his own press clippings. Slocum reached into Payson's
inside vest pocket, then drew in a sharp breath of air and
whistled. Fast Johnny, like the man Slocum had killed
back in the cantina, as well as the one in the hotel, was
carrying a great deal of money with him. The one in the
cantina had had a hundred dollars, the one in the hotel
over eighty, and Fast Johnny had a little more than a
hundred. If this kept up, Slocum thought in amusement,
he would wind up recovering all the money owed him
for the horses . . . though this certainly wasn't the way
he wanted to do it.

Slocum climbed out of the ravine and threw down
rocks until Fast Johnny was completely buried. It wasn't
a fitting burial, perhaps, but better than leaving him out
for the varmints.

Slocum wondered about Rawls. Rawls was a right
smart son of a bitch, and now he had Slocum boxed in.
Someone watched him, someone knew his every move.
Rawls's men were getting chewed up but, according to

Billy, there was yet another man on Slocum's trail. Who was the other one?

He chewed on it, felt the answer scratch at his brain, but the name wouldn't come to him.

15

Slocum trailed Billy for a little while. Then he saw that Billy was heading away from the border, probably trying to lead Slocum away as well. All right, Slocum thought, let Billy have his fun laying down false trails. He had a lead anyway. The boy had mentioned Duermequi. The hardcase he'd shot back in Paso Corto was on the way to meet someone in Duermequi. Well, that particular gent wouldn't be able to make the meeting, but maybe Slocum could make it for him. Slocum left Billy's trail, backtracked in a wide circle, then picked up the trail for the village of Duermequi.

Duermequi was no different from any of the other Mexican towns he had ridden through in the past several days—a dozen or more adobe buildings scattered around a large square. This village did happen to have a church, though, a large mission which stood guard at the south end of town. The shadow of the cross fell across Slocum's face as he rode into the churchyard. The padre was drawing water from a well and Slocum got down and walked toward him. The priest wore a brown cassock held together with a strip of black rawhide, from which dangled an oversized wooden crucifix. A bald spot shined from the top of the priest's head. The hair around the bald spot was gray.

"Hello, Padre," Slocum said in a friendly tone.

The priest nodded, studying Slocum closely.

"I'd be obliged for a drink," Slocum said. "The water in my canteen's grown a little stale." Slocum pulled out ten dollars in green and handed it to the priest.

"This is God's water," the priest protested, waving the money away. "It is free."

"The money isn't for God's water," Slocum replied easily. "It's for His church."

The priest smiled. "Bless you, my son," he said, taking the money.

Slocum plunged the dipper into the bucket and scooped up the water, then drank long and deep. It was cool and delicious, and he drank until his belly was full. Then he wiped his mouth with the back of his hand.

"Would you like to fill your canteen?" the priest asked.

"Yeah, thanks," Slocum said. He lifted the canteen from his saddle, poured out the old water, and began refilling it with fresh, pouring the water from the dipper. "Padre, I'm looking for some men . . . some Americans."

"Friends of yours?"

"Not exactly."

"I see."

"They'd have a Mexican girl with them," Slocum went on.

"I know of no such men," the padre said.

"You sure? They're all ridin' purebred black horses—

beautiful creatures. You can't miss them."

"Well now," the priest said nodding. "It so happens there is such an animal in the village now, but he is not being ridden by an American."

"One of the villagers owns such a horse, does he?"

"No. This is not an American, but he is not of this village. I do not know him, but he seems to be a most unpleasant person."

"He could be one of the men I'm looking for," Slocum replied, as he put the top of his canteen, then slipped it back onto his saddle. "They have a Mexican riding with them. Would you have any idea where I might find this man?"

"So you can kill him?"

"What makes you say that?"

"You have death about you," the padre said. "You have death in your eyes."

"Padre, these are evil men. They murdered many men and women down in Santa Luz. Now they have an innocent young woman, Linda Soltano, as their prisoner. If I don't find them soon, I'm afraid they'll kill her too."

"You have already killed some of these men?" the priest asked.

"Yes," Slocum admitted.

"And you intend to kill more?"

Slocum sighed. "I don't want to kill any more," he said. "All I want to do is get the girl back safely. But if I have to kill again to do that, I will."

The priest looked for a long moment into Slocum's eyes, and Slocum felt a little shiver pass over him. It was disconcerting to have someone look inside you that way, all the way to your very soul. He felt as if he were standing naked with all his past sins, actual and conceived, bared to the priest's gaze.

"I believe you," the priest finally said. "You have death in your eyes, but I do not see pleasure in the killing. Not like the pleasure I see in the eyes of the man you are seeking."

"The man with the purebred horse?" Slocum asked.

"*Sí.* He rode in two days ago. Already he has killed two men. He eats but he does not pay for the food. He drinks, but he does not pay for the wine. He defiles the women, he mocks the men, and no one stops him, because all fear him."

"Where is he?" Slocum asked.

"He is in the cantina."

"*Gracias,*" Slocum said. He hooked his canteen on the saddle pommel, then looked back at the priest before he mounted.

"Padre," he said quietly, "I want to talk to that man, ask him about the captive girl. But, if he is like the others I have tracked, he'll try to kill me as soon as he sees me. If that happens..."

"I know, my son," the padre said. "You'll have to kill him." The priest made the Sign of the Cross. "*Vaya con Dios,*" he said.

"Obliged." Slocum mounted, nodded his head at the priest, then rode toward the middle of the town.

A dog ran out as if to challenge Slocum's horse. It darted in and snapped once at the horse's hooves, then ran back out of the street and barked from the safety of the corner of a building. Slocum crossed the town plaza and tied his horse to the hitching rail in front of the cantina. There, at the next hitching rail, was another of the purebred geldings he'd brought down from Texas. He walked over to the horse and patted it gently.

"Hello, fella," he said. "Remember me?" He looked at the horse's rump and saw the Soltano brand. Whoever had ridden this horse was inside, and whoever he was, he was one of the people Slocum tracked. If he came from the Soltano ranch, he was obviously involved in the massacre that had gone on there.

Slocum drew his pistol and looked toward the door just as a customer came outside. The patron saw Slocum standing in front of the cantina with a drawn pistol and he hastened his step to move quickly out of the way. Then he stopped in the shade of the building next door and looked back toward Slocum.

"The hombre that rode this horse," Slocum asked, "is he in there?"

"*Sí,*" the frightened customer replied, nodding his head. "He is a very dangerous man, *señor.*"

"Thanks for the warning," Slocum said dryly. He took a deep breath, then stepped inside.

Evidently, Slocum had been seen coming. Everyone in the cantina moved out of the way to stand up against the walls. The middle of the place was open and all the tables and chairs were empty except for one Mexican who sat on a chair in the middle of the room, facing the door. On the Mexican's lap was a pretty young girl. The expression on the girl's face showed stark terror. The Mexican was using her as a shield, Slocum realized immediately.

"Let the girl go," Slocum demanded.

"You die, Slocum!" the Mexican answered as he stood and raised his pistol to aim at Slocum. That was a mistake, because at that moment the young girl slid off the man's lap to the floor and out of the line of fire. That gave Slocum a clear shot. He took it without hesitating for an instant.

The girl screamed as two pistols roared. Slocum heard the shatter of glass as the Mexican's bullet crashed into

a bottle on a nearby table. The shot was wild, because
even as he was pulling the trigger the Mexican was dead.
Slocum put a ball right between his eyes. The Mexican
fell backwards, crashing through the table. Glasses and
bottles tumbled from the broken table and from one of
the bottles, tequila spilled and merged with the blood
which was already puddling on the floor. The gunsmoke
drifted slowly up to the ceiling, then spread out in a
wide, nostril-burning cloud. Slocum looked around the
room quickly to see if anyone else might represent a
danger. He saw only the faces of the customers and they
showed only fear, awe, and, in some cases, even thank-
fulness.

"*Gracias, señor,*" the girl said, shaking visibly. "*Gracias.*"

"*Sí, señor,*" the bartender added. "He was an evil
man."

Slocum walked over and stared down at the man he
had just killed. He recognized him, but this wasn't the
man he'd expected. This was Luis Ortiz, Delgado's man.

Slocum holstered his pistol, then bent down to go
through Ortiz's pockets. He found almost two hundred
dollars. Slocum gave twenty to the bartender.

"Bury him," he said. "Buy yourself a new table."

The priest came in and looked at the dead man. He
kissed his stole and dropped to his knees.

"You gonna say words over him?" Slocum asked.
"He's a killer."

"Even the lowest sinner is a child of God," the priest
replied softly.

Slocum handed the priest the rest of the money he
had taken from Ortiz's body. "You said he killed a couple
of men. Did they have families?"

"*Sí,*" the priest answered.

"Divide this up between them," Slocum said.

"They will be most grateful, *señor*."

Slocum looked at the girl who had been sitting on Ortiz's lap. She was crying softly, but he knew it was from fear, not from sorrow.

"This man's name was Luis Ortiz," he said. "He and six Americans murdered many men down in Santa Luz. They also took a young woman and they're holding her prisoner. I'm looking for the others. Did this man say anything about them, or the woman?"

The girl shook her head.

"He said nothing to me, *señor*," the girl answered.

"How about the rest of you?" Slocum asked. "Anyone hear him say anything about his partners? About a prisoner?"

One of the Mexicans spoke quietly, apologetically, his head bowed as if he were intruding. He spoke in Spanish.

Slocum looked at the priest, hoping he would interpret for him, but the priest was praying softly. Slocum looked to the girl for help. "What'd he say?"

"He said the dead man asked him how far to Eagle Pass," the girl answered.

"Eagle Pass? On the border?"

"*Sí*. Do you know this place?"

"That's the way I came down." Slocum looked at the Mexican who had spoken. "Tell him I said thanks. His information might save a young woman's life."

The girl spoke to the Mexican, and the Mexican beamed, proud that he had been of service to the *gringo* who was the avenging angel of Duermequi.

Slocum saw another little piece of cloth about a mile south of Eagle Pass. It had been quite a while since Linda left any sort of a trail marker. Slocum figured either she was being closely watched or she was running out of cloth. This piece hung on the limb of a palo verde tree. He picked it up and examined it, satisfied himself that it was from Linda's dress, and breathed a small sigh of relief. At least she was still alive.

Slocum felt as relieved as he was trail-weary. For a moment his attention drifted off. He didn't even hear the bullet that hit him. He felt a sudden, numbing, sledge-hammer blow to his arm as the bullet's impact knocked him from his horse. Immediately, a man jumped down from a nearby rock and ran toward him, firing a rifle from his hip, jacking a new shell into the chamber and firing again. The bullets hit the ground around Slocum, zinged off the rocks, and filled the canyon with a whining sound.

Slocum had been hit in the left arm, and had fallen on his right side. As a result he was lying on his right gun and, because his left arm was temporarily numbed, was unable to draw that one. Finally he forced himself to roll over onto his left side, banging his wounded arm painfully against the rocks, while he pulled his right pistol. By the time he managed to get it out his attacker had closed to within three feet of him. Slocum fired just as the man raised his rifle for one more shot. The bullet tore into the man's throat. The man gagged, dropped his rifle, and put both hands to his throat. Slocum saw blood spilling between the man's fingers as he shot again. This time Slocum's bullet hit the man right in the middle of the face, tearing away his nose.

As the man dropped, Slocum stood up and looked around for a second assailant. He heard a horse riding away and quickly climbed up a nearby rock formation to try to get a shot.

Too late. Whoever it was was well out of range by now. But Slocum knew he would be waiting on the other side of the border.

Waiting to kill.

16

Texas.

The United States.

Home.

It wasn't home like the red hills of Georgia had once been home. But it was as much home as any place could be for Slocum. It was home because of language, even though there were nearly as many Spanish-speaking people in this part of Texas as there were English-speaking Americans. It was also home because the attitude of the people here shared much of Slocum's own attitude. He knew that Americans in general, Texans in particular, wouldn't let another man gain control over them the way Soltano controlled the peons on and around his ranch. Texans possessed independent souls.

"I say there," Slocum had once heard an Englishman address a cowboy, "would you be so kind as to summon your superior for me?"

"My superior?" the cowboy replied, squirting a stream of tobacco between the Englishman's feet. "Mister, that son of a bitch ain't been born yet."

Slocum chuckled as he recalled that comment. Let the philosophers write and the politicians speak—one simple statement said it all as far as Slocum was concerned.

The lay of the land changed sharply on the United States side of the border. The barren, rocky hills gave way to open, brush-covered prairie. It was good cattle country, but as far as Slocum was concerned it was good for something else too. In this country there would be very little likelihood of an ambush unless the ambusher used the cover of darkness to make his play.

Slocum knew that the man he trailed realized that as well, so, expecting a night ambush, Slocum put his bed-roll and saddle out to provide a silhouette in the dark. The trick had worked for him before—he had no reservations about going to the well again. After he put out the bedroll, he lit a small campfire, then moved about twenty yards away and waited.

Slocum wished for a smoke, but a smoke might give his position away, so he put the thought out of his mind. He sat there in the dark with his gaze sweeping back and forth, looking for any movement. He had learned long ago that he could see better in the dark by not looking directly at an object, but off to one side.

He wondered where Linda was, wondered about her safety. Had Rawls hurt her? Had he . . .

Slocum never should have left her at the ranch when he went over to see Delgado, he scolded himself again. Something had told him then that he was making a mistake. But she had insisted on staying to see to the burial of her family, and how could Slocum deny her that? He, too, had lost his entire family and knew what it was like to be alone in the world. He had lost everyone in the War—a loner now, and had been for some time. There were moments when he would give anything for the right to be like other men—to have a home, raise a family, make a contribution to society. But he also thought of the vulnerability of such a life and realized he was leading the only life he could ever lead. He couldn't be emotionally hurt because of anyone else, and more importantly, no one else could be hurt because of him.

It had been a long, tiring trip. Slocum dozed during the night, but even while asleep, he kept alert. When a small pebble was rolled out of place by someone advancing on foot, Slocum was instantly awake.

According to the position of the stars, Slocum knew it was well after midnight. He sat very still and looked around slowly, not concentrating on any one spot. Using this sweeping technique, he detected movement—a silent shadow slipping through the darkness. Too far away to see the intruder's face, Slocum could tell by the way he walked who the man was. It was the same man who had delivered Rawls's proposition to him, the man Slocum shot in the hip. He called himself Billy, Slocum remembered, and Billy was favoring his hip as he walked.

Billy limped forward slowly, then stopped about five yards away from Slocum's bedroll. Slocum watched as he eased his pistol out and pointed toward the empty blanket. He fired two shots into the blanket, the muzzle flash of his pistol lighting up the night.

"Get out of that, you son of a bitch!" the man yelled.

"I'm over here, Billy," Slocum stated in a cold tone, standing up suddenly.

"What? Slocum!" Billy shouted. He spun around and began blazing away in Slocum's direction. Slocum returned fire, using the twelve-inch-wide muzzle-blast as his target. Billy dropped his gun, then crumpled. Slocum walked over, looked down at him. Even though there was only moonlight for illumination, Slocum could see the wounds clearly—one in the stomach and the other in the chest. The one in the chest was already frothing, and Slocum knew his bullet had opened a lung. He heard the sucking air from the chest wound.

"You've killed me," Billy said.

"I guess I have," Slocum answered gently.

"I should've ridden away when I had the chance."

"Yes, you should've," Slocum agreed, holstering his pistol.

Billy coughed. "Fast Johnny Payson was gonna be such a big man, kill you hisself," Billy said. "I thought maybe I'd go back to Rawls and tell him I took care of it for him."

"Where is Rawls?"

"I don't know."

"Why don't you tell me Billy? What's in it for you now? If I get there in time, I might be able to save the girl."

"I don't know," Billy answered weakly. "Honest . . . I don't." He started coughing. "Can I have some water?"

Slocum walked over to get his canteen. He knew about this, about the terrible dryness in the throat just before a man died. He had given many men a last drink of water during the War, and quite a few since that time. Many of those, like this one, were people he'd killed.

Slocum knelt down and handed his canteen to Billy. Billy took several desperate swallows, making gurgling sounds as he drank.

"Mosca," Billy said when Slocum finally pulled away the canteen.

"What?"

"Mosca," Billy said again. "I'm s'posed to meet someone in Mosca."

"Rawls?"

Billy couldn't answer right away, because he suddenly erupted into a fit of coughing. Finally, the coughing stopped.

"Billy? Billy, is it Rawls you're supposed to meet in Mosca?"

There was no answer.

"Billy?" Slocum put his hand on the man's neck. There was no pulse.

"Shit," he mumbled. Slocum stood up and put the top back on his canteen, then walked over to his saddle and pulled out a small spade. The soil was fairly easy to dig; within half an hour, he'd dug a shallow but serviceable grave. He rolled Billy in, covered the hole with dirt, and patted it down.

Slocum had left six graves between him and Santa Luz.

Slocum slept for a couple of hours and was underway again before daybreak. As he watched the rising sun streak the eastern horizon with bars of red, he thought about Rawls. He knew now that Rawls had some reason to keep Linda, and he would never have exchanged her for any reason. Slocum was close now; only two men left, Rawls and the Mexican. He wondered which one was waiting in Mosca.

The little outpost town of Mosca, Texas, was quiet when Slocum rode in about noon. A mixture of American and Mexican cultures, the town reeked with the spicy aromas of Mexican cooking and American pastries. He could smell coffee, pork chops, fried potatoes, and baking bread.

"Linda? Linda?" a woman called. Startled, Slocum jerked his horse to a halt to look in the direction of the call.

"Yes, Mama?" a little girl's voice answered.

"Bring me the other basket of clothes, will you, honey?"

"Yes, Mama."

An American woman was hanging clothes on a line in the back yard of her house, and a young girl, about twelve, came off the back porch carrying a basket of wet clothes. The woman, startled by the fact that Slocum had stopped his horse, looked at him nervously and took a step backwards. Slocum touched the brim of his hat in greeting, then urged his horse on.

Though the town was laid out American-style—a row of false-front buildings facing the street, rather than adobe structures gathered around a square—most of the people Slocum saw were Mexican. It was noon, and many of them were taking their *siesta*, though some sat or stood in the shade of the porch overhangs. A game of checkers was being played by two gray-bearded Americans in front of the feed store, watched over by half a dozen onlookers. A couple of them looked up at Slocum as he rode by, his horse's hooves clumping hollowly on the hard-packed earth of the street.

The American shopkeeper who ran the dry-goods store, obviously not recognizing *siesta* time, came through his front door and began vigorously sweeping the wooden porch. His broom did little but raise the dust. He brushed a sleeping dog off the porch, but even before the man went back inside, the dog reclaimed its position in the shade, curled around itself comfortably, and was asleep again within moments.

Slocum saw the horse from the far end of the street.

It was impossible not to recognize the animal—the powerful chest and shoulders, the sleek legs, the graceful withers of a purebred. And yet, he also noticed that something was wrong. Something he couldn't put his finger on from this end of the street. The horse seemed defeated. He couldn't understand that. He had never seen a purebred look defeated.

Slocum rode slowly down to the far end of the street, then tied his horse to a hitchrail next to the purebred. He walked over to the animal and patted it on the neck. The horse's coat was smeared with foam and it was breathing in labored gasps. Its muzzle and the hitchrail were flecked with blood which had spewed from its mouth and nostrils with each painful breath. The horse was slowly and painfully dying on its feet. Slocum still hadn't seen a purebred defeated: this animal hadn't been defeated, Slocum cursed to himself, it had been destroyed. Someone had ridden it until its lungs burst.

For an instant, Slocum felt a savage rage in his guts toward any person who would do that to a horse, to any horse, especially to one like this fine animal—a beautiful horse he had picked out and delivered himself.

"Sorry, fella," he said softly. "I didn't know what I was gettin' you in for, or I would've left you where I found you."

Slocum sighed, then pulled his pistol and aimed at the horse's head. The horse looked toward him, its big brown eyes sad and knowing. The horse nodded once as if telling Slocum that he understood what had to be done. The purebred looked away then, as if waiting stoically for release from its suffering. Slocum pulled the trigger, and the horse thundered to the ground. The gunshot echoed through the quiet streets for a long time. Then all was silent.

Rarely had Slocum pulled the trigger feeling a heavier heart than he felt at that moment.

The gunshot awakened several people from their outdoor *siestas*, and they raised up and looked toward the saloon, toward the big man with the smoking gun and the horse which lay motionless on the street.

A curtain fluttered in one of the false fronts.

A cat yowled somewhere down the street.

A fly buzzed past Slocum's ear, did a few circles, then descended quickly to the horse, joined almost immediately by a dozen others, drawn to the bloody feast.

Slowly, deliberately, Slocum rammed the empty hull from the Colt's cylinder, and slipped in another cartridge. He fit the pistol back into the holster, then his boots rang on the steps leading up to the boardwalk.

Slocum strode into the saloon.

17

Slocum pushed through the batwing doors, then stepped to one side so that the wall was at his back. At the bar, a pail of beer in front of him, his moustache dripping with moisture, stood an old friend. A better word would be acquaintance. Slocum and Pedro Gallinas really never did become friends during the time they rode together, bringing the purebreds down from Texas.

Slocum was not surprised to find Pedro. He had known for some time now that Pedro was the Mexican who had burned the buildings south of the border. Pedro was also the one who had fired at him in Santa Luz. And, Slocum noted, he wore a brace of .45 caliber pistols. That answered the final mystery. Pedro was the one who had sent him the bullets.

"Hello, Pedro," Slocum said. His words were cold, flat, and menacing.

Pedro didn't turn around, didn't even look at him in the mirror. Instead, he stared into his pail of beer. "So, you have found me, eh, *amigo?*" Pedro asked. "And now one of us must die, no?"

"No, not one of us. You, Pedro. You're going to die."

There were half a dozen drinkers at the bar. At Slocum's words, they hurried to move away. Tables and chairs scooted across the floor as everyone else in the saloon got up and moved back, out of the line of fire.

Slocum caught the movement of the others out of the corner of his eye. He believed Pedro was the only one of Rawls's men here, but he wanted to be sure, make certain that Pedro didn't have a friend planted in the crowd. He saw no one who represented any danger to him.

"What were you shooting at out front?" Pedro asked.

"I had to shoot your horse."

"You should not have done that. He was a good horse."

"Not after you got through with him, you horse-killing son of a bitch."

Now, Pedro turned away from the bar to face Slocum, both hands on the butts of his pistols, his legs spread apart. "It's my horse, *señor*. I do what I wish with my own horse."

Moving slowly, Slocum pulled the three bullets from his shirt pocket. He tossed them onto the bar in front of the Mexican.

"What is this?" Pedro asked.

"They have my name on them. Maybe you want to put them in your pistols before you draw."

"I already got one with your name on it, *gringo*," Pedro answered, and, even as he spoke, he started pulling his pistols free of their holsters.

It was here now—the moment of truth. All the posturing and gesturing was over. Slocum felt a strange sense of exultation as his hand snaked down to his side to draw a single pistol. He was fast, faster than he had ever been before, and he had time to take quick, deliberate aim and shoot Pedro in the gut. The Mexican, the barrels of his .45s just topping the holsters, pulled the triggers of both pistols, shooting lead into the floor. A red stain began to spread just over his belt buckle.

Pedro's guns clattered to the floor and he put his hands over his belly and watched the blood spill through his fingers. Inexplicably, he smiled.

"Carajo, you are fast, *señor,"* he said. "Faster than everyone told me, faster than I thought. I did not know you were so fast, *mi amigo."* Pedro weaved back and forth for a moment, then pitched forward, crashing through a table before landing on the floor.

Smoke from the discharge of the three weapons formed a big cloud, which began to drift toward the ceiling. Bootsteps rang on the front porch and two men came running in.

"What happened?" one of them shouted. "What's going on?"

Slocum turned his gun toward the door, and the two men who had just run in, both Americans, threw their hands up.

"Jesus, mister! Don't kill us!" one of them shouted.

With a sigh of disgust, Slocum lowered his pistol.

"Christ, Adams, you ought to know better than to come bargin' in like that," one of the men in the saloon said. "You're lucky you didn't get your fool head blowed off."

"You know this here Mex you shot?" another asked.

Slocum didn't answer. Instead he knelt beside Pedro, who was still alive.

"What's it all about, Pedro? Money?"

"Much money," Pedro rasped.

"Not for you," Slocum said. "Not any more. Why did you take Linda?"

"Ah, there is much more, *gringo*."

Suddenly it was all clear to Slocum. He stood up and rammed his pistol back in his holster.

The batwings swung open again and a man with a badge came inside. His hair and moustache were gray, his face lined around his blue eyes. There was a sharpness to his eyes which told Slocum that the peace officer had probably been pretty good when he was younger. Only age had driven him to a backwater town like Mosca. Age had undoubtedly slowed the man down, but Slocum imagined there were a few who had made the mistake of misjudging him. Slocum didn't intend to make that mistake.

"You shoot the Mex?" the man with the badge asked.

"Yes," Slocum answered.

"Wanna tell me what it's all about?"

Pedro laughed. "Sheriff. Do not blame my *amigo*. If he had not killed me I would have killed him."

"The Mex is right, Sheriff," one of the witnesses said. "The Mex drew first. It was a pure case of self-defense."

"You shoulda seen it, Sheriff," another offered. "It was the fastest thing I ever seen in my life. The Mex started for his guns, then you couldn't see no more than a shoulder jump and this here fella was spittin' lead afore the Mex had even cleared leather."

The sheriff sighed and looked at Slocum.

"Did you have to bring your grudge to my town?"

"Sorry, Sheriff. This is where I caught up with him," Slocum replied.

"Yeah, well, if there's anything I don't need around town it's a gunfighter." The sheriff sighed again. "I'm not even going to check to see if there's paper on you, mister. I just hope you aren't plannin' on stayin' too long," he said, squinting at Slocum. "Fact is, I'd take it right kindly if you'd just get on out now."

"That's exactly what I've got in mind," Slocum informed him.

"*Hombre*, wait," Pedro called to Slocum. "We are *amigos, señor*. You aren't going to leave me like this, are you? You took pity on my horse. Do the same for me. Kill me quick."

"Fuck you, Pedro."

Slocum stalked out of the saloon. He knew that Pedro would die, and the death would be slow.

Linda lay on a cot and stared at the ceiling above her, trying to focus her thoughts. She tried to concentrate on where she was, on how long she had been with this man who seemed to control her every move. He told her when she should ride and when she should rest, when she could eat and when she could sleep. It seemed as if he had always been in control of her life . . . as if she had no memory of the time before she was with him.

Who was he? she wondered to herself. He wasn't her father. He wasn't her husband. Why did he have such control over her?

Several times over the past three days Linda had tried hard to come up with the answers, to find out where she was and why she was here. And why she couldn't leave. There were no answers, because she had been given something to drink, days earlier, and the drink had dulled her mind, numbed her senses.

It had been some time now since she drank any of the potion, and her periods of lucidity were more frequent and of longer duration. Gradually she was beginning to gather her scattered thoughts together and make some sense out of what had happened to her.

She remembered, vividly, the scene at her home... her father and brother dead, all the loyal hands killed, Filomena shot before her very eyes. She had expected to be shot as well and was surprised when she was taken and forced to leave with those men.

Linda could remember little about the past three days. Snatches of memory came to her... hours of riding in the hot sun and through the dark of night, the anger of the man named Rawls as he learned that, one by one, his men were being killed off.

She could also recall a night of pleasure, of giving herself to a man... but not the man who was with her now. As she lay in the cot, a warmth came over her and the face of the man floated before her.

Slocum. His name was John Slocum, and she remembered too that Slocum was trying to help her, had been with her just before the bad men came.

Where was John Slocum? she wondered in desperation. Was he dead? Had he been killed like the others?

Linda began crying softly, and she was still crying when Dave Rawls came into the room carrying a tray with steaming beans and a cup of coffee. He set it on the table beside her bed. Rawls was a big man, not tall and not fat, but big, with wide shoulders, a barrel chest, and muscle-knotted legs and arms. His hair was dirty blond, his eyes pale blue. He didn't wear a beard, but he often went several days without a shave so that there was a ragged growth on his chin and upper lip.

"I thought you might be hungry," Rawls told her. "Here's some beans, a little coffee."

"I . . . I'm not going to eat or drink any more," Linda answered him.

Rawls chuckled. "I know what you're thinkin'," he said. "You think I got somethin' in it to keep you knocked out, don't you? Well, I only did that while I was movin' you. I got you where I want you to be now, and truth to tell, I need you with all your senses. Don't worry, there ain't nothin' in the food or the drink. Here, I'll show you."

Rawls ate a spoonful of the beans and smacked his lips appreciatively. He drank a swallow from the coffee cup.

"See?" he said, grinning. "It's all right. There ain't nothin' wrong with it."

Linda sat up on her cot and began eating. She couldn't remember the last time she had eaten anything, yet she knew she must have been fed during the last few days. Still, the beans tasted unusually good to her, and she ate with relish.

"Now, that's what I like," Rawls said with a chortle. "I like seein' a woman eat like she enjoys it."

"Where am I?" Linda asked.

"Texas," Rawls answered. "Laredo."

"Why am I here?"

Rawls chuckled again and held up his hand. "Don't you be worryin' your pretty head about that," he said. "You'll find out everything in time."

"Why have you done this? Why did you kill my father and the others?"

"Your old man was a stubborn son of a bitch," Rawls said. "He tried too hard to hang on to his money. If he'd just turned it over to us like we asked, he wouldn't have got hisself kilt."

"That's a lie," Linda protested. Vividly now, she could recall the scene of her father sprawled in front of the safe—and the safe open. "The safe wouldn't have been opened if my father hadn't opened it for you."

"Well, now, I guess you got me on that one," Rawls admitted. "But the truth is, we're after a little more than what he had in the safe."

"My father had a small fortune in that safe," Linda protested.

"That's the thing about small fortunes," Rawls grumbled. "You get a little one, the next thing you know you want a great big one. I'm afraid your papa was just in the way."

"And Filomena? And the others?"

"Well, they was in the way too, I reckon," Rawls told her. "The only thing I regret is I didn't kill Slocum too."

Linda drew in a sharp breath and looked up at Rawls. "You mean John is still alive?"

"Yeah, he's still alive. He's killed off all my men, but he's still breathin'."

Despite her situation, Linda smiled broadly. "He's still alive," she said thankfully.

"You believe he's gonna come after you, don't you? You think he's gonna rescue you?"

Linda didn't answer.

"You don't have to answer. I know that's what you been countin' on. I'm countin' on it too, if you wanna know the truth."

"You want him to come after me?"

"Sure do," Rawls answered, grinning boldly. "He's a pretty hard man to track down 'n' kill on his own. Seems like the only way I'm gonna get the job done is to set me a little trap for him. And when you set a trap, why, you need some bait. You, my pretty little *señorita*, are the bait."

Linda shuddered.

18

It was late afternoon as Slocum approached Laredo. He could hear the occasional sighs of steam from a train which sat on the track at the depot. He rode alongside the track, following it toward town. When he reached the edge of town, he rode past the green, red, and brass engine which sat on the tracks, steaming and popping like a giant teapot. The fireman and the engineer were both on the ground beside the engine. The fireman was oiling bearings with a long-snouted oil can, while the engineer supervised. They both looked up as Slocum rode by.

The train was a freight, so there were few people on the station platform. Had it been a passenger train, Slocum knew the platform would have been full.

"The freight clerk around?" Slocum asked.

The engineer raised up and wiped his face with a red bandanna. The action only served to move the soot around and did nothing to reveal the features of his blackened face.

"I seen 'im in the freight office yonder, oh, not more'n a mite ago," he answered, pointing toward the office.

"Thanks." Slocum continued alongside the line of freight cars toward the platform. The building which housed the ticket office and waiting room was the dominating structure of the depot, the freight office having been relegated to a smaller building which sat at the far end of the platform.

Slocum rode to the front of the freight office, then climbed down from his horse. A man rushed out of the little building carrying a sheaf of papers in his hand.

"You the freight clerk?"

"Yes, sir," the man answered back over his shoulder. "I'll be right with you. I've got to get this train dispatched."

"Take your time," Slocum responded.

Slocum saw a pump at the end of the building, and he walked down to it and gave the handle a couple of jerks. Then he held his head under the spout to let the water run over him. When his head was thoroughly drenched, he raised up and wiped his face with his kerchief, smoothed his hair with his fingers. The splash of water felt good, revived him somewhat from the long ride, but he could have used an entire bath.

The engine whistled two long whistles, signaling that the brakes had been released and the train was about to roll. Steam hissed from the relief valve, slack was taken out of the couplers, and the wheels began to turn. Slocum watched for a moment, then the freight clerk returned, almost in as much of a hurry as he had been when he rushed out to the train to give the crewmen their orders.

"Now, sir, what can I do for you?" the clerk asked.

"Would you like to arrange for a shipment?"

"No," Slocum answered. "I want some information."

The clerk looked at Slocum for a long moment as if the tall man had just asked an embarrassing personal question. "Does this look like an information bureau?" his eyes seemed to ask. But he only sighed and pointed inside.

"Sure, why not?" he replied. "I need to get off my feet for a few minutes anyway. Come on in, drink a cup of coffee with me. Anything I know, I might be able to tell you."

"Thanks," Slocum said. "I appreciate that."

Slocum followed him inside the little building and took a seat when it was offered. While the clerk poured them each a cup of coffee, Slocum looked around. A big clock told him it was six o'clock in the evening. A calendar on the wall indicated that the date was July 3rd. The picture on the calendar showed a passenger train crossing a high trestle somewhere in the Rocky Mountains. A night view, the train's lantern beam and the bright moon lit up pine trees and snow-covered peaks. Every window of every car shone with a bright, golden lantern glow. A pleasant picture. Slocum found himself wishing he could be on that train going somewhere . . . maybe San Francisco. It had been a long time, he thought to himself, since his last visit to that city.

The clerk put a cup of coffee in front of Slocum, then sat down across from him.

"Now," he said, sucking the steaming hot coffee through his lips. "What can I do for you?"

"I hope you can give me the information that will save a girl's life," Slocum answered in an even tone. "Have you ever heard the name Soltano?"

"Soltano? Jose Soltano? Sure I know him. Everybody

knows him. He's got a ranch just north of here."

"Jose?" Slocum asked, surprised. When he asked the question, he'd been thinking of Linda Soltano. Slocum leaned back in his chair for a moment and thought about the possibilities of another Soltano. "Could be Jose," he said to the clerk. "Does he have a relative who is a big-time rancher down in Mexico?"

"Sure does. It's his brother. Fact is, I think he's a don or something. You know, one of them Mexican titles? I never did get it quite straight what his whole name was."

"Don Eduardo Honorio Velazquez y Soltano," Slocum told him.

The freight clerk laughed. "That's it," he said. "It's a mouthful, but now that I recollect, that's exactly what it is. Yeah, he's Jose's brother, all right. I've heard Jose talk about him."

"Jose and his brother are close?" Slocum asked. The answer to the mystery climbed out of the void for Slocum. No longer quicksilver, he could grab hold of it now—make sense out of what had been bothering him. He needed only confirmation, and he believed the clerk could give him that.

"No, sir, I wouldn't say they was close at all. Fact is, I get the idea there's bad blood between them," the clerk said. "I remember a year or so back when the drought hurt ever'one 'round here pretty bad. Jose tried to borrow some money from his brother."

"Did he get anything?"

"Not a peso," the clerk replied. "I don't think the don even answered. Jose went on a rampage, talkin' about how half the money was rightly his anyway, how his brother had cheated him out of his inheritance. Swore he'd get even."

"Did he?"

"Not that I know of. Fact is, Jose's been pretty quiet here lately. I haven't seen him in a couple of months. His foreman, Pedro, used to come in now and again to arrange for a cattle shipment or something, but I don't even think he's been around in several weeks."

"Pedro? Pedro Gallinas? A short man?"

"Yeah, that's him, all right," the clerk agreed. "Sort of a sour fella—I mean, the kind you wouldn't want to get riled. Wears a brace of .45s and he's got that look about him like he knows what to do with 'em." The clerk studied Slocum for a moment. "Kinda like you, mister. Oh, not that you're of a mean disposition or anything, but I'd lay wages you're a man gets his way about most things."

Slocum finished his coffee and stood up. "Much obliged for the coffee, and the information."

"Don't know as I gave you anything you couldn't of got anywhere else," the clerk said. "You mentioned somethin' about savin' a girl's life. I sure don't think I helped you there."

"You helped me a lot more than you think," Slocum assured him, but gave no indication of explaining more. The sound of a distant train whistle floated in through the open window. Even with the big Waterbury clock on the wall in front of them, the clerk pulled a watch from his pocket, opened the case, and looked it over.

"That'll be the six-thirty, eastbound," he said. "Mostly passengers, but I reckon there'll be some express freight for me."

"You say Soltano's ranch is just north of town?"

"Yes, ask anyone. You can't miss it."

Slocum walked outside with the clerk. The train approached from the west, silhouetted against a sky smeared in colors—orange, red, and deep blue. Smoke from the engine billowed up in a rolling black cloud, steam from the cylinders purpled in the fading light and drifted away. The headlamp was already lit and made a bright pinpoint of light against the front of the engine.

Slocum mounted and rode downtown, stopped in front of a cafe. He longed for a good meal. Besides, he wanted to visit Soltano's ranch.

Slocum ordered fried pork chops, potatoes, and scrambled eggs. The young copper-haired woman who served him smiled and dropped a few hints that she would be available after work, if he took a liking. Without being rude, Slocum let her know that he wasn't interested. All he wanted to do now was eat his supper and sort out all the information.

Slocum realized that he'd been set up, that Pedro had contacted Rawls in Fort Worth to arrange the whole deal. They wanted Soltano's money, all right, and Delgado's too, but Pedro had said there was more. If there was more money, Slocum reasoned, that could only mean one thing. Finally Slocum knew why they'd kept Linda alive, after killing everyone else, and why they still needed to keep her alive.

Linda was not only an orphan now, she was the only survivor. That meant she was next in line. She would inherit everything—the ranch, the businesses in town . . . and, most importantly to Rawls and Jose Soltano, the rest of the don's money. Don Eduardo had told Slocum that he kept his money in the bank in Mexico City, and yet there was a hundred thousand dollars in cash at the ranch. If he had that much at the ranch, Slocum figured, he might have as much as a million dollars sitting in the bank in Mexico City.

Slocum shook his head sadly. One man's greed had

cost the lives of so many others. He wondered if Soltano's brother was a twin.

The waitress came to clean off his table.

"Is there a place where I could take a bath?" Slocum asked.

The redhead smiled. "How about my place?" she teased. "I could scrub your back for you."

"That sounds like a good offer," Slocum agreed, "but I'm in a hurry. If I let you scrub my back, I may never get finished."

The woman laughed. "You've got that right, mister." She pointed across the street. "But, if you've got no yen for what I can offer, the barbershop has a place in the back. You can get a bath there."

"Thanks."

Slocum paid his bill. Fifteen minutes later he settled into a tub of hot water. He had a feeling Linda was being held at the Soltano ranch, and when he went for her, he wanted to go clean.

For the first time since her capture, Linda was aware enough to study her surroundings. The room she was in was barren except for the cot she was lying on, the table alongside, and one chair. There was not another stick of furniture in the room, not even a carpet on the floor. The window was draped with black curtains, and when she got out of bed and walked over to pull the curtains to one side, she saw that the shutters were closed so she couldn't see outside.

Despite the fact that the room was barren and the windows blacked out, there was something about the room that was vaguely familiar, and she tried hard to fix it in her mind. Then, as her head flopped to one side, she studied the tiny rose pattern on the wallpaper, and she knew what it was. She had seen that wallpaper before. She had been in this room. But when? And where was it?

Linda tried hard to capture what was turning over in her mind. But the harder she tried to concentrate, the more it seemed to slip away. She sat up and studied the wallpaper more closely. It would come to her, she told herself. It had to come to her.

Linda heard the bolt being thrown on the door behind her. She quickly turned around to look.

The man who entered the room was no stranger.

"Uncle!" she gasped at the sight of her father's brother.

Jose smiled at her. "You have nothing to fear, my dear. I'm here to look after you now."

"Oh, Uncle Jose, I'm so glad you're here." She sobbed with relief, believing she'd been saved. "It's been terrible. You've no idea what I've been through."

Jose put his arms around her, and Linda, thankful at long last to be with someone who could protect her, went to him with the joy of one who is being rescued.

"There, there," Jose said. "It'll soon be all over, you'll see."

"Can you take me out of here?" Linda asked.

"Yes, yes, of course I can," Jose answered. "Soon. Just as soon as you sign some papers."

Linda looked up at him in surprise. "Papers? What papers?"

"Nothing. Just a few loose ends that need to be cleared up about your father's estate, that's all."

"Can't . . . can't all that be taken care of later? Uncle, please, don't you understand? I've been held prisoner here . . . I've been given some sort of potion to dull my senses. I've . . ." Linda stopped in mid-sentence. Her uncle had left the door open, and beyond the door, on the wall outside, Linda glimpsed a painting of her grandfather. She recognized it immediately, because her father had one just like it in his home—in her home. Now she knew where she had seen the wallpaper before. Now she knew where she was.

"Uncle Jose!" she gasped. "This is your house. You . . . you are one of them!"

Her heart sank with a new and dreadful fear.

19

"So, she's figured it out, has she?" Rawls said, stepping into the room and facing Jose. "I told you she would. You should've let me do it my way in the first place."

"We tried things your way," Jose answered angrily. "Your way seems to be to kill everyone. That was not my plan."

"I changed the plans," Rawls said with a sly smile.

"Perhaps so, *señor,* but you didn't plan on John Slocum, did you? Now it seems that John Slocum has killed all of your men."

Rawls's smile widened. "Well, now, ain't that a shame? From my way of lookin' at it, that just leaves more money for you and me."

"And what assurance do I have, *señor,* that you will not decide to kill me, and take my share?" Jose asked nervously.

"Oh, I couldn't do that, Soltano," Rawls explained. "You're the goose that's layin' the golden eggs. If I kill you, I get nothin'."

"See to it that you remember that," Soltano warned.

"Course, on the other hand, if I ever think you're tryin' to double-cross me, I'll kill you deader'n shit," Rawls threatened.

"Don't worry, *señor,* you will never catch me double-crossing you."

Rawls chuckled. "You didn't listen good. I didn't say *catch* you, I said if I *think* you are doin' it. See, I ain't no jury. I don't have to have nothin' proved to me. All I gotta do is believe you're holdin' out on me and I'll kill you. You savvy that?"

"*Sí, señor.*"

"Good. Now that we got all this straight, let's get the girl's name on the papers and get it over with."

As Linda listened to the conversation, she realized with a growing sense of horror that her uncle was behind everything. The murder of her brother and her father, even of Filomena, was all the doing of her uncle. She had thought her father was an evil man, but not even his actions could equal Jose's brutality.

"Come on into the dinin' room, girl," Rawls ordered. "We got some papers we want you to sign."

"I'm signing nothing," Linda answered, her eyes glaring in hatred.

Rawls let out a long sigh. "I'm goin' into the dinin' room," he said to Jose. "I'll give you two minutes to change the girl's mind. If she ain't in there by that time, I'm goin' to start breakin' her toes, one by one. And if that don't do it, I'll break her fingers, until I leave her just enough bone to write her name."

"Linda, please," Jose begged her. "Do not be a fool.

Don't you see what kind of man this is? He'll do anything he needs to get what he wants. You heard what he said. And if he can't get you to sign that way, he'll kill you. That's what he is—a killer."

"How can you tell me he is a killer when you are just as bad?" Linda asked. "You are behind all this."

"No," Jose said. "I didn't want to kill anyone. I only meant to trick your father into giving me what is rightfully mine. I had no idea it would go this far."

"You should have known what would happen when you associated with a man like *Señor* Rawls," Linda challenged.

"Am I different from Eduardo? Did your father not hire the same *Señor* Rawls for his war with Delgado?"

Linda looked sharply at her Uncle Jose. He was right, her father did hire Rawls and his killers for his war.

"Look what happened to my father," Linda reminded him. "How do you know that won't happen to you?"

"It will not happen because Rawls needs me," Jose replied. "And he needs you. He needs you to grant me the power of attorney to act in your name."

"And after I sign the papers granting you the power of attorney, will he still need me?" Linda asked. "Or will he kill me?"

"He will still need me," Jose answered. "I will watch out for you."

Linda chuckled, a dry, mirthless chuckle. "Somehow, Uncle, I don't find that very reassuring." She sighed, then decided to try to buy as much time as possible. "Where are these papers I am to sign?"

Jose smiled broadly. "They are in the dining room," he said. "Come, let's sign them and end this terrible ordeal."

Linda followed her uncle down the hall to the dining

room. Rawls stood by the dining table. On the table, in the light of a lantern, she saw an inkwell, a quill pen, and some papers. She walked over to the table and picked up the papers to look at them. One was a will naming Jose Soltano as her beneficiary. The others were legal documents giving her Uncle Jose power of attorney.

"This is a will," she said, her expression changing from surprise to a look of horror. "If I sign this, I'm leaving everything to you."

"It means nothing, my dear," Jose said, trying to sound reassuring. "It's just a formality."

"It means I'll be dead before the ink is dry," Linda blurted out.

"No, no," Jose insisted. "Trust me. I will take care of you, I promise."

"Just as you took care of the rest of my family?" Linda asked. Tears welled in her eyes, streaked down her face. Suddenly she felt very, very tired. She sighed, then sat at the table and reached for the quill pen.

"That's a good girl," Rawls enthused.

The night air felt cool as Slocum rode through the dark streets of Laredo, fresh from a bath and a shave. Laredo was bigger than any of the villages he had traveled through in recent weeks, and this fact was most noticeable to his ears. Instead of one saloon, Laredo boasted of four, and as Slocum rode through town, he could hear piano music and laughter spilling from each one of them. From certain parts of town the sounds blended into a cacophony of noise, but as he passed each saloon in turn, the sound coming from within would enjoy a moment of superiority over the others, so that he could actually identify some of the songs or make out a few of the more loudly spoken words.

On the outskirts of town, a handful of kids playing hide-and-seek renewed his faith that some people still lived normal, settled lives, without having to check every shadow or size up every stranger.

The freight clerk was right when he had said everyone in Laredo knew Jose Soltano—for good reason. As the town of Laredo fell off behind him, Slocum passed under a gate which identified the land on both sides of the road as Rancho Soltano.

He rode on for at least a mile before reaching the main house. Of course, it was more than just a house—a compound with a bunkhouse, cookhouse, smokehouse, granary, barn, equipment shed, and the big house. All the buildings were dark, except the bunkhouse and the big house.

Slocum dismounted, left his horse hobbled about one hundred yards away, and approached the compound on foot. He slipped through the shadows until he was outside the bunkhouse, then he edged along the bunkhouse until he could look through one of the windows.

A heated game of cards was going on inside the bunk-house, and just about every cowboy was involved in the action. There was only one who wasn't playing or watching—he was lying on a bunk looking at a mail-order catalogue. Most were Mexican, though Slocum saw a few American wranglers. He didn't recognize anyone, and none of them looked like anything more than working cowboys. That was good; he didn't want any surprises when he went up to the main house.

Slocum darted from the bunkhouse over to the sprawling hacienda, again keeping to the shadows. He slipped along an outside wall until he reached a lighted window. Then he peered inside.

Linda sat at a table in the dining room. An American

and a Mexican stood over her. With a quill pen in her hand, she was leaning over a sheaf of documents. An inkwell was positioned a few inches from her writing hand. Light from a coal-oil lamp bathed her face, made her black hair shine. He spotted tears beneath her eyes and streaks next to her nose. A muscle twitched in Slocum's jaw.

She looked sad, frightened, but otherwise healthy. That pleased him. Earlier, once he'd figured out what Rawls had in mind for Linda, he had stopped being too concerned about whether or not she would be alive, but he did concern himself about what they might be putting her through. From the looks of her, she hadn't been beaten or physically abused, but Slocum knew there were other forms of torture.

Slocum walked around back, then up onto the porch. He worked the latch on the door, found it was unlocked. Carefully opening the door, he stepped into a room. From the rich smells of recently cooked food, he knew it had to be the kitchen.

A crack of light spilled into the kitchen from the far side. Slowly, quietly, and with both pistols drawn, Slocum stalked through the kitchen, following the crack of light until he reached a hallway. The light came from a door at the opposite end of the hall, and he knew that was the dining room. He stepped quietly down the hall, and heard Linda's voice, trembling with emotion.

Slocum stepped into the room. "You must be Rawls."

"What the—" Rawls shouted in surprise. Rawls and Jose both whirled, hands plunging for their pistols.

Slocum shot Rawls first, with the pistol in his left hand, then swung his other pistol toward Jose, firing point-blank at the man's gun hand. Rawls went down, clawing at a hole next to his heart. Jose screamed in pain and doubled over. Slocum stepped in close, sent the toe of his boot square into the man's scrotum. Jose fell to the floor, writhing in agony.

Linda stood up, her face blank with shock. She rushed toward Slocum and came into his arms. He held her around the waist and drew her close.

"I never thought I'd see you again, John Slocum."

"Were you really going to sign those papers?" he asked.

"I had no choice."

"They would have killed you, even so."

"I know. But I would have had the last laugh."

Slocum looked at the papers. On the line for her signature, Linda had written not her name, but *"Vayate con el diablo."*

"What does that mean?" he asked her.

"It means something like—go to hell."

They both laughed. "Well, Jose will hang first, but likely he'll wind up there." Slocum eased the smoking pistols back into their holsters.

Slocum walked over to the window and cut down the cord which opened the drapes. He came back to Jose, who was moaning in pain and covered with sweat, and began tying him with the cord.

Suddenly three men ran into the room, guns drawn. One was an American.

"What is it? What happened?" the American blurted out. "Heard shooting from down at the bunkhouse." With Rawls dead and his boss being hogtied by Slocum, the man raised his gun. "Who the hell are you, mister?"

"Put the gun down or you won't live to hear my answer," Slocum replied. Both Slocum's pistols were in his holsters, and the cowboy had the drop on him, yet there was enough certainty in Slocum's voice to convince the cowboy that he could back his words.

"All right," the cowboy said nervously. He put his pistol on the table and motioned for the other two men to do the same. When the three pistols were on the table, they stepped away from them without having to be asked.

"I think the girl can explain it best," Slocum offered.

"Pancho, Jesus, you both know me," Linda said, excitedly.

"*Sí,* since you were little girl."

Quickly Linda told the story, how her family and all the hands at her father's ranch had been killed, how she had been brought here as a prisoner and forced to sign papers which would turn everything over to her Uncle Jose. One of the hands killed back at her father's ranch was Pancho's brother; he was saddened, then angered by the news.

"Mister, the only question I got is why you left the son of a bitch alive," the American said when Linda had finished her story.

"I'm willing to let the law handle that," Slocum said. "I'd appreciate it if you men would go get the sheriff, though."

"We'll have him out here pronto," the American promised, and the three men left to tell the others what had happened and to go get the sheriff.

"I owe you much, John," Linda said when the others were gone.

"You owe me nothing," he told her. Slocum pulled the money from his pocket that he had taken from the six dead men. He took out his share for the horses and shoved the rest across to her. Jose's eyes flared with fury as Linda stood on tiptoes, ringed Slocum's neck with her arms, and kissed him hard on the lips.

"Maybe I do owe you something," she whispered. "Something money can't buy."

"I'll accept that," he said huskily.

JAKE LOGAN